OH, COME ALL YE DRAGONS
A VALKYRIE BESTIARY HOLIDAY TALE

KIM MCDOUGALL

Oh, Come All Ye Dragons
Copyright © 2022 by Kim McDougall
All rights reserved.
Published by Wrongtree Press.

Cover and book design by Castelane.
Cover art by Kayla Schweisberger.
Editing by Elaine Jackson.

Paperback ISBN: 978-1-990570-14-8
eBook ISBN: 978-1-990570-13-1

Version 2

FICTION / Fantasy / Urban
FICTION / Fantasy / Paranormal

About This Book

The Inbetween is full of magic, monsters and marauders. But it's also full of booty, if you know where to look. And Roden & Hogg Reclamation Services knows just where to find those resources that are so scarce and valuable in the post- Flood-War era.

But when dragons nest on a copper reclamation site, who do they call? Kyra Greene. No pest too large or too small.

Now Kyra must leave home days before her baby's first Christmas, for a three-day trek into the wilds. Can she convince a stubborn dragon queen to move her nest before the scavengers brings in the guns?

Kyra Greene's new adventure into the Inbetween turns into a rollicking girls' weekend away and brings her face to face with some old friends even as she comes out of her comfort zone to make new ones.

Oh, Come All Ye Dragons, A Valkyrie Bestiary Christmas Tale takes place after the events of Book 6, *Ghouls Don't Scamper*.

Also By Kim McDougall

Valkyrie Bestiary Novels
Dragons Don't Eat Meat
Dervishes Don't Dance
Hell Hounds Don't Heel
Grimalkins Don't Purr
Kelpies Don't Fly
Ghouls Don't Scamper

Valkyrie Bestiary Novellas
The Last Door to Underhill
The Girl Who Cried Banshee
Three Half Goats Gruff
Oh, Come All Ye Dragons

Hidden Coven Series
Inborn Magic
Soothed by Magic
Trigger Magic
Bellwether Magic
Gone Magic
Hidden Coven: The Complete Series

Shifted Dreams Series(Writing as Eliza Crowe)
Pick Your Monster
Lost Rogues

CHAPTER

1

I was thumbing through recipes for gingerbread cookies, pumping milk, cooking sweet potato mash for the baby, and thinking of a dozen other tasks that needed doing, when out on the lawn there arose such a clatter, I dropped my widget on the table, tore open the shutters and threw up the sash. The moon on the breast of the new-fallen snow…

Oh, screw it. My new ward was fighting with the goblin twins.

Again.

There was no moon. Only blood on the mangled snow along with hats, gloves and boots flung off by three tussling boys.

I sucked in a deep breath to yell at them, and the milk bottles harnessed to my chest by the pumping machine clanged together. I wasn't dressed for outside eyes. My nursing blouse barely covered me.

I leaned my forehead against the cool window. My head hurt. My boobs hurt. I hadn't showered in days. Christmas seemed more like work-work-work than ho-ho-ho this year.

I knew I had only myself to blame, but that didn't make things easier. I wanted everything to be perfect. Baby's first Christmas only came once. At six months old, Holly wouldn't remember it, but I would.

I threw a sweatshirt over myself, harness and all, then flung open the back door.

"Raven! Get inside now!" I yelled in my best mom voice. Three startled faces looked up. They were red from the cold. Tums's nose was bleeding. "Tums, Tad, get cleaned up and find your sister. She'll expect a good reason for fighting. Again!"

I slammed the door making sleigh bells on the wreath jingle and the bottles hanging from my chest jangle. *Oh, what fun it is.*

Raven and the goblin twins hadn't outgrown their squabbles. And over the summer, Raven had grown a good six inches. This seemed to make Tums and Tad more determined than ever to best him in a wrestling match. But today—before the battle in the snow—the shrieks had been only squeals of delight as the kids zoomed down the hill beside the barn on sleds made from old shovels.

Add to the Christmas shopping list: sleds for the boys.

A hiss from the kitchen told me a pot had boiled over. I rushed to the stove. Milk bottles swayed. The night-jaguar yowled as I stepped on his tail. Sorry Grim! I skidded on the wet spot in front of the stove, grabbed the pot lid without an oven mitt, and dropped it just as quickly.

"Damn!" Steam and bits of broccoli hissed around the stove's flame. I sucked on my singed fingers and turned off the burner. Inside the pot, the blackened broccoli stuck to the bottom. I sighed and wished Dutch hadn't asked for two weeks off. He'd been taking care of Mason—and now me—for years. Dutch never burned the broccoli. He did everything with a calm efficiency that I couldn't imitate.

I dumped the pot in the sink. There was no salvaging that mess.

Homemade baby food from home-grown produce had sounded like a good idea six months ago. But six months ago, I'd been as big as a house and had nothing to do all day while I waited for our little Holly to arrive. I'd made grand plans. Homemade food from all organic produce. Breast milk for the first year at least—I adjusted the pump that had come loose in my mad dash across the kitchen and was now making a sucking noise like an open chest wound—and I'd even made baby clothes, though I couldn't sew in a straight line. And, of course, I would continue to work at least part time. I wasn't ready to give up my identity as CEO of Valkyrie Pest Control.

But some days, it all seemed a bit much.

And now Christmas was only a week away. So gingerbread cookies.

I sipped my tea, wishing it was coffee, and flipped through the recipes on my widget. None looked easy. Shouldn't cookies be easy? Maybe I could buy gingerbread cookies? Just this once. Holly was too young to eat them anyway, right? But there was Raven and the goblits to think about. This was our first Yule season all together. I wanted it to be special.

The baby monitor cackled. That was the problem when you lived with an alchemist. Mason and Raven had spent hours in the lab tweaking the store-bought monitor so the baby's cry sounded like a witch rubbing her hands over a boiling cauldron. When she cooed, the monitor brayed like a manticore. Hilarious.

"I'm coming, baby girl!"

I pulled off the sweatshirt and checked the bottles. They were only three quarters full. That wouldn't do. I had a full afternoon of critter wrangling, and my stock of milk was low. I resigned myself to another fifteen minutes of pumping, and headed toward the bedrooms.

Our house was mainly one big open space that we called the great room in a throwback to when the manor had served as an inn. The great room was living room, dining room and office space all in one. The kitchen and breakfast nook flanked the sunnier southern side. On the other end, a hall led to our bedrooms and upstairs guest bedrooms. A massive circular hearth dominated the room. Grim sat in front of it, washing a paw. His hooded gaze told me I wasn't yet forgiven for stepping on his tail, though his pride had probably suffered the worst wound.

I was nearly to the hallway when Mason stepped out with Holly in his arms. She was pouty and red-faced from sleep. Wisps of blond hair stuck to her sweaty cheeks. She was sucking on one fist. The other grasped a fistful of Daddy's hair.

Mason looked at my frazzled state. His eyes landed on the milking machine strapped to my chest and he grinned.

"Moo."

"Ha ha. That's funny every time." I pulled off the pumps and adjusted my shirt to cover myself. "I have to work this afternoon. I want to make sure that Gita has enough milk." During the afternoons that I worked, my banshee nanny had been watching Holly with the help of Suzt, one of the goblits.

I returned his assessing gaze. "I thought you didn't have to go into the city today?"

7

Mason was half dressed. He wore dark dress pants and no shoes. His muscular chest stretched a white undershirt to its limit. Maybe my post-natal hormones were in overdrive, but by the gods, there was nothing sexier than a man in an undershirt holding an infant.

He smiled as if he could read my thoughts. He probably could too. After a long forced abstinence, we'd recently rekindled our intimacy in the bedroom, and I couldn't get enough of that dark-haired, silver-eyed man.

"You're leaking." His eyebrow quirked upward. I looked down to see a wet stain blossoming across my shirt. I crossed my arms, but that did nothing to hide it. He tugged my arms down.

"The sight of you making milk to feed our daughter is the most beautiful thing in the world." He tucked one of my braids over my shoulder. It was coming loose and little hairs stuck to my neck.

"Go have your shower," he said. "I've got breakfast." He tweaked Holly's nose. "Don't I, little Holly berry. Papa's going to make you *un déjeuner delicieux!*"

Holly half-cooed, half grunted, and jammed her face against Mason's shoulder, smearing it with baby tears and snot.

"Group hug." He pulled me in. I wrapped my arms around them both. Despite the mess in the kitchen and the hundred things on my to-do list, there was no place I'd rather be.

"Someone smells like barf," I said, pulling away. Mason craned his neck to peer over his shoulder. I turned him around. Yep. A big stream of barf down his back.

"Whoop!" He lifted Holly high in the air. "Clean shirt first. Then breakfast!"

And we all headed back to the bedroom to clean up and face the day.

CHAPTER

2

ven driving to work was a new experience. Roy, my scrag mechanic who'd kept my old truck running by sheer will for the last ten years, had finally refused to fix it.

"Can't even use it for parts, really," he'd said, scratching his thin beard. "The motor is running on oil and prayer as it is."

I wasn't ready to give it up entirely, so the truck was parked behind the barn. Arriz, our goblin estate manager used it for hauling branches, garbage or whatever else needed doing around the property.

I drove a new van now, a fancy contraption full of alchemical add-ons like self-tinting windows and auto-drive. Mason insisted it was the safest vehicle on the roads. To me, its best features were the baby seat in the back and the locked cage full of tools and weapons behind that. I was a modern, working mom.

The console was more complicated than a jet plane's from before the wars, but unlike Mason who preferred to feel in control while driving, I was happy to let the car drive itself. The twenty-minute journey from Dorion Park, where our house lay in its hidden glade, to Sayntanne and my office was just about the only down time I had these days. I set the car's stereo to play a mix of country-rock from the early millennium and sat back to enjoy the sounds of my nearly forgotten youth.

But down time also meant time to worry. Had I left enough milk for Gita? Holly had still been red-faced when I left. Was she coming down with something? There's no better champion of guilt than a new mom leaving her infant to go to work.

But in truth, I enjoyed my few hours away from home every other day. It was a sort of gleeful joy, like playing hooky and not getting caught. Then, I redoubled my guilt for feeling happy at being away from my baby.

Sigh.

No one told me that motherhood would be a series of never-ending internal negotiations.

I pulled into the lot in front of Valkyrie Pest Control and parked by the garage that had been turned into a makeshift gym and weapons locker.

Emil's car filled one of the other three parking spots. My vampire assistant lived in my old apartment behind the office. A second car was parked beside his—a sleek black compact. This would be our mysterious new client, Carmen Perez-Malone. She was a site manager for Roden and Hogg Reclamation services. She wouldn't give Emil any details about the job over the phone, saying that it was confidential. I'd researched R&H Reclamation last night and was impressed. They scavenged goods in the Inbetween but went after the big stuff like fuel, scrap metal and other resources that were hard to manufacture in the post-war world. The Inbetween was a risky place to work and R&H Reclamation had their own militia to protect their sites and workers. It was quite an operation. I was curious about what they would need my services for and why they were in such a hurry.

Inside, Emil was entertaining our new customer. Ms. Perez-Malone stood when I entered. She was easily six-feet tall. She greeted me with a wide smile. Her skin was a dusky bronze. She had wide-set brown eyes and flaxen hair that fell to her shoulders in corkscrew curls.

"Ms. Greene." She reached me in two strides—her high heels clicking on the tile floor—and held out a hand. I shook it and my hand disappeared within her large grip. At five-feet-eight and still carrying some baby weight, I wasn't a small woman, but standing next to Carmen Perez-Malone, I felt tiny.

"Please, call me Kyra."

"Perfect. And I'm Carmen."

"And please excuse me for being late."

"Oh, yes, Emil was just telling me you have a new baby at home. How delightful."

Her smile was genuine, but somehow, I didn't believe Carmen thought babies were delightful. She was dressed in a blouse and skirt that was just a bit too short for standard office attire. Her manicured nails shone with perfect, red gloss. They weren't the nails of someone who made baby food and gingerbread cookies.

She returned to her seat and folded one long leg over the other. She didn't wear nylons and didn't need them. Her legs were smooth and brown and without blemish. When I wore a skirt, I had to wear opaque tights just to cover the scars and bruises.

Despite her size, Carmen pulled off the chic business look with sleek grace. Jealousy wasn't normally one of my vices, but I glanced down at my worn work pants and flannel shirt with a little less comfort than normal.

Emil brought us steaming cups of tea. He made it dark and bitter, but it still couldn't compare to coffee. I made a face and put the cup down.

"Sorry, our coffee rations were cut again."

"We all have to make sacrifices these days." Carmen waved away my concern, but she took only one small sip before setting the tea down too.

"So how can we help you?" I asked.

Carmen laid a trim black case on her lap, opened the silver clasps and handed me a sheet of paper with the Roden & Hogg logo embossed on the top. A bunch of legal jargon filled the rest of the page. I looked at it with surprise. She handed another to Emil. As he read it, his eyebrows rose so high they were lost under his mop of curls. Carmen saw our reactions and smiled.

"It's a standard nondisclosure agreement. We put it on paper so there's no electronic trail."

Interesting. I rubbed the sheet between my fingers. It wasn't real paper, but even synthetic was expensive these days.

"Do you need a pen?" Carmen held out a ball point pen and pulled off the cap with a smile. "You press this end to the paper."

"Thanks. I know how to use a pen." I just hadn't seen a disposable one in over fifty years. The scavenging business had its perks.

I read through the NDA. It was standard legalese stating that anything discussed here in connection to a possible consultation job with Roden and Hogg Reclamation services was strictly private, including any information about R&H excavations and bulla sites.

That part was interesting. No one really understood how or why bullas appeared, only that in the years right after the Flood Wars, Terra took back much of the land. Entire towns were swallowed by foliage, landslides and shifting land masses. But once in a while, Terra spat part of the old civilization back out like a time-capsule of another era. A bulla could be a single house or an entire village, and it usually erupted from the ground perfectly preserved, as if the people once living there had just stepped away.

Large reclamation companies rarely bothered with them, but bullas were priceless to homesteading scavengers who picked them clean of medicines, furniture, gasoline and anything else they could use. The big companies spent their money on excavations, looking for industrial sites that could be repurposed. If they were interested in a bulla, it had to be a big one.

The last paragraph of the NDA threatened law suits, fines and even jail time for leaking any R&H secrets.

I finished reading it to find Emil watching me with a curious smile. He did love a good drama.

I put the paper down on my desk and tried to order my thoughts.

"Can I ask how you heard about us?" I said. "We're pretty small time and this," I waved at the NDA, "seems big time."

"On the contrary. Valkyrie Pest Control has quite the reputation. You've a long history working for Hub, I understand." Carmen's frank gaze assessed me and I nodded. "I also interviewed representatives from the three parliamentary parties before coming here. The fae, in particular, had nothing but praise for your work."

Two years ago that wouldn't have been surprising, but since Merrow took over as Prime Minister, my relations with the Winter Court had been strained.

And if Carmen had interviewed reps from Hub, that could mean this job had military implications. I really didn't want a job with the military.

"But the most valuable recommendation came from Avalon Moodie."

Now that was a surprise. I'd met Avie last year. She was the hedge witch I'd gone to see when I found myself inflicted with a disease-curse that endangered my pregnancy. Apart from being a witch, Avie was the mother a brood of kids from fifteen down to toddler-age. Since I had just become an instant parent with the arrival of Raven in our lives, Avie had taken me under her wing in the mom club. Mostly we drank wine, ate pastries and complained about our kids, our bodies and our jobs.

"You know Avie?" I asked.

"Sure, we were besties in high school. I went the corporate route, and when Avie started pumping out babies, we sort of lost touch. But I met Trevor on a job site a couple years ago and we reconnected."

Trevor was Avie's husband and an active soldier in the Hub Militia. His job was a constant source of anxiety for Avie because it took him outside the ward to protect our food supply from marauders. He'd been on the front line of the godling attacks for the past year.

If Carmen had met him on a job site, it confirmed that R&H only took on high value reclamations. On the other hand, Avie and Trevor were good people. If Carmen had their endorsement, I at least had to listen to her proposal.

Oh, what the hell. All the NDA had done was make me more curious anyway. I took the pen and signed my name at the bottom. Emil did the same.

Carmen took the papers and tucked them back into her case. She folded her hands over her lap and favored me with a smile that was calculated to charm and pacify all at once.

"Now, tell me what you know about dragons."

CHAPTER

3

"I read your blog," Carmen qualified, "so let's assume I know as much about dragons as was printed there." Her perpetual smile died and she fixed me a stony gaze. "What I want to know is what you didn't put on the Ley-net."

I sipped my bitter tea and said nothing. Most people have trouble with silence and rush to fill it. Carmen wasn't one of those. She watched me carefully and quietly, until I finally had to pull the information from her.

"First, tell me why you would even bother with dragons."

"Because they're squatting in a copper factory—a bulla that appeared last spring. We can't access the copper without a serious fight."

This was starting to sound like a kill mission. I set the mug down and returned Carmen's gaze.

"First, I want to be clear. I am not an exterminator. As a lover of all creatures, big and small, wild and tame, I would urge you not to kill the dragons. And if that's what you're looking for, you'll have to find someone else."

"But there isn't anyone else who has actually spoken to a dragon." She let that little bomb drop with a sly smile. "Yes, I read the debriefing transcripts from the opji uprising. I did my homework before coming here."

She really did. Those transcripts had been sealed. Two years ago, Alvar, the brother of Leighna, Queen of the Fae and Prime Minister of the Fae Party, had staged a coup with his supposed allies, the opji vampires. Of course, the opji had murdered Alvar as soon as his usefulness had run out. That's what vampires did. The young prince had been a fool to trust them. His death had given those in charge the opportunity to white-wash the whole affair. The story leaked to the general public was that Alvar had been kidnapped by the opji and forced to help them.

In the weeks after the attack that had left dozens of Hub officers dead, I spent many hours in debriefing. My statement included details of my involvement, going right back to finding the enslaved thunder of dragons and fostering Ollie, the stunted baby dragon who hadn't been able to fly away after I freed the others. The little dragon became the McGuffin that unraveled Alvar's entire sordid plot.

And somewhere, in my statement, I must have mentioned that Ruby, the red queen, used mind-speak to communicate with me.

"Look, I'm going to lay it all out," Carmen said. "We don't want to kill the dragons. Not unless we have too. But we need to negotiate with them. They're occupying a bulla that R&H legally claimed."

"Careful," I said. "Your hubris is showing. No one can really claim the Inbetween. No one but Terra."

Carmen cocked her head, as if re-evaluating me. "Huh. I didn't take you to be a Terran fanatic."

"Not fanatic. I've spent a lot of time in the Inbetween. Call me a realist. If you found something valuable, it's only because Terra decided to spit it out. And she can swallow it back down whenever she wants."

"That's exactly why we need your help and in a hurry. We've tried to trade with the dragons, but there's nothing we have that they want," Carmen said.

"Because you're offering the wrong trades. Dragons eat magic. You need to get your hands on as many magically-rich artifacts as you can."

Carmen brightened. "See you're already a valuable asset to the team. When can you leave?"

"I can't go anywhere! It's less than a week 'til Christmas, and I have a six-month-old at home."

"We'll make it worth your while." She pulled out another piece of synthetic paper, wrote a number on it, and handed it to me.

My heart screeched to a halt. That was a big number.

Emil leaned over my shoulder to read it and whistled. "Must be a lot of copper."

"Copper we can get anywhere." Carmen waved a hand. "This bulla is an entire, intact, pre-war copper wire manufacturer. Its warehouse holds raw copper, but more importantly it has thousands of coils of annealed copper wiring, already jacketed and ready to use. Do you have any idea of how important this find is? There is enough wiring in that bulla to build communication networks to Argentina and back!"

That was something special. In the post-wars world, copper cabling was particularly valuable because it took to magic better than the glass fiber optic cables that had been so popular at the turn of the millennium. But Terra had collapsed all the copper mines, making them too dangerous to excavate. A factory full of ready copper was worth more than gold.

"How did you claim it if the dragons were already there?" I asked.

"They weren't. Our scouts found it last spring, but the paperwork just came through for our official claim in November. We'd left a patrol to guard the bulla against homesteaders, but we didn't think there'd be trouble. There isn't much in the factory worth taking except the copper, and the average homesteader would have no way of hauling or selling it."

"So what happened?"

"We lost contact with the guards about the same time our claim was approved. We sent a team to investigate and they found a herd of dragons living there. We can't get near the site."

"A thunder," Emil said.

"What?"

"A group of dragons is called a thunder."

Carmen smiled at him like he was a cute puppy who had just piddled on the floor.

I folded the outrageous offer and slid it across the table toward her.

"I can't go. It's too close to Christmas. I have a family." I had milk bottles to fill and diapers to wash.

But Carmen was used to getting her way. "What if I promise to have you back in time. In fact, we'll give it a week tops. After that, we'll go to plan B."

My guts rumbled. I already didn't like the sound of plan B. No one else would advocate for the dragons if I didn't go. R&H Reclamation would send in their militia with blasters blazing.

"I'll go on two conditions."

Carmen cocked her head, the way a hawk does when it's trying to get a better look at its prey.

I counted my conditions off on my fingers. "First, I have to okay it with my babysitter. And second, I get half up front. Non-refundable if the dragons don't negotiate."

"Done." Carmen gave the desk a gentle pound with her fist, and I realized I should have negotiated for more. She opened her case and produced another piece of synthetic paper, another contract that would never appear on the Ley-net. "Welcome to the team."

f I was leaving in two days, I had errands to run before returning home. I skirted around Abbott's Agora, the sprawling outdoor market, and took the northern route into the city, along the old Highway 40. It was the only major artery that still linked the city center with the outer reaches of the ward, and it was mostly intact.

Much of the city had been destroyed during the Flood Wars, and the magical shield that protected Montreal had decimated any structure taller than ten stories. Ward planners and alchemists had spent big budgets to clear the debris from Highway 40 just after the ward's inception, but they hadn't cleared the remains of the ill-fated rapid transit train that ran alongside it.

Work on the skyway train had begun in 2018, but wasn't finished before the flash bombings of 2025 that left the city dark and in ruins. The skeletal remains of the skyway rose beside the highway like the bones of a long dead sea serpent. It was an ominous sight that always gave me a little shiver. Today was no different and the cement leviathan reminded me of the danger I would be putting myself in when I ventured into the Inbetween. I'd seen real sea serpents. And water dragons. And a fire-spitting chimera, man-eating sasquatches, carnivorous bison…If you could imagine it, the Inbetween grew it—bigger and badder.

What right did I have to take such a risk now? It wasn't just my life endangered now. Okay, Little Bean had graduated to Holly and she no longer rented out my womb, but that didn't mean she needed me any less. The gods knew, even a short trip into the Inbetween could end in disaster, and then what? Holly would grow up never knowing her mother. And Mason? He'd sworn to never give his heart away again, but he had. For me. And for Holly.

I slammed on my brakes. The light in front of me was red. I hadn't even seen it. The driver behind me leaned on his horn and gave me the finger. I sat at the intersection, gripping my steering wheel and shaking. I should have put the damned car on auto-drive.

The light turned green and I turned into a parking lot that was boxed in by several large stores. One of those was Rick's Wilderness Gear. If I was going outside the ward in December, I needed some good winter gear. And with Carmen's deposit in my account, I could afford it.

TWO HOURS LATER, the trunk of my car was full with top-of-the-line hiking gear and a few alchemical luxuries like a heated sleeping bag that rolled up smaller than a t-shirt.

I drove home worrying about what I'd say to Mason. How could I tell him I was leaving our baby a week before Christmas? I worried about over-taxing Gita—she wasn't as spry as she used to be—and whether I had enough milk for Holly in the freezer.

Carmen's contract was folded in my shirt pocket. It felt as heavy as all the gold it was worth.

It was dark already and snowing when I parked my van beside the house. The barn doors were open, and I decided to check on my critter charges. I zipped my jacket against the cold and made the trek across our parking lot to the barn. The snow was already ankle deep. Dekar, the oldest of the goblin children stood on a ladder beside the open barn door with a hammer in hand to fix a shutter on the window above the door. He saw me struggling through the snow.

"Don't worry, Miss Kyra. We'll have that cleared as soon as it stops snowing."

I waved to him. "I know you will."

Mason and I had met Dekar and his family when they were trying to gain access to Montreal as refugees. Dekar's mother had died in the InBetween and his father, Arriz, decided they'd had enough of the homesteader life. But visas to enter the city weren't easy to come by. Mason had offered Arriz a job as estate manager. We lived close enough to the city that the ward provided some protection. And with the gargoyle Guardians living on site, we were as safe as a family living in the Inbetween could be.

Since then, I'd hired Dekar's younger brothers, Muzzy, Tak and Gibus to help care for my various odd rescues.

The goblits were sweeping old wood shavings from the cages when I entered the barn. They piled the dirty bedding outside the door. In the spring it would be shoveled into a trailer and spread in a field where I was trying to grow grass suitable for grazing so we could keep horses. In the post-Flood-Wars world, horses were much more reliable than cars.

"You're doing a good job," I said to Gibus who was the youngest and still thought cleaning out the barn was a treat.

"The leeches are having babies!" he shouted a bit too loud.

"Take it easy," Muzzy said as he wheeled out another barrow full of dirty bedding.

"How long until they hatch?" the younger goblit asked.

"I'm not sure, I've never seen leech babies before." The new vampire leeches would be a welcome addition. More than once, they'd saved me time on a pest control job. And I was almost as excited as Gibus to see the hatching. Of course, I might miss it now.

I crouched down to Gibus's level. "I'll make you a deal. If I get you a widget, will you record the egg hatching? I want you to take a video every day. And make notes about the changes you see. Can you do that?"

"My own widget?" His eyes were big enough to swallow the moon.

"It'll be a loaner, so you'll have to take good care of it." I knew that Arriz wouldn't let the children accept such an expensive gift. "And I expect detailed reports on the leech eggs."

Gibus nodded. His sister Suzt would appreciate my suggestion. She was always looking for ways to incorporate reading and writing into the younger goblits' everyday life.

"Good. Now what else is going on?"

Muzzy took over the updates. "Everyone is fed and the cages are clean. We're nearly out of crayfish again." I made a note to order more. "And I'm worried about Kur."

"Is something wrong with him?" I asked. My ice-sprite could be temperamental, but he usually flourished at this time of year when cooler temperatures meant he didn't have to sit on a bowl of ice all day.

"I'm not sure." Muzzy's face scrunched up in concern. "But you should have a look. He wouldn't eat today, and even Hunter can't cheer him up."

"Hmmm." That was unusual. Keeping the critters caged wasn't ideal, but for their safety, they couldn't be left to wander the Inbetween. I tried to give each of them free time in the barn and outside when weather permitted. Hunter, my pygmy kraken, did a good job of amusing himself and the more sentient critters like Kur. If the kraken wasn't pretending to be an acrobat by hanging from the ceiling beams, he was splashing water from his tank or tossing his toys around the barn. And Kur loved to egg him on.

Today, Hunter watched from the depths of his tank. His face was pressed to the glass, eyes wide and sober. Only one tentacle stretched over the tank's rim.

Across the aisle, Kur was curled in a ball in his cage with his back to the rest of the world. I reached in and tickled his fur right below his wing. He back twitched, but he didn't look around.

"Hey buddy, you feeling okay?" I reached for the basket of maple-flavored treats beside his cage. Kur had a sweet tooth. I waved the cookie under his nose. Nothing. I picked him up and turned him over. He slitted his eyes and yawned. His wings flared in a stretch. He gave a little chirping purr and tucked his head under my chin. He was cool to the touch as an ice-sprite should be. My fingers roved through his fur, looking for bumps or bruises. He didn't cry out, so nothing hurt.

I put him back in the cage and offered the cookie again. This time he took it in one of his strangely human hands. He plopped onto his butt with his feet sticking straight out and munched the treat.

"Is he okay?" Muzzy was peering around my shoulder.

"I think so. Let's keep an eye on him for the next few days."

Of course, I wouldn't be able to do that because I'd be gallivanting in the Inbetween. What a terrible time for a road trip.

I left the goblits to their work and headed for the house. Mason was working at his desk while the baby slept in her playpen beside him. Grim watched over them from his favorite spot by the fire. When I came inside, his eyes opened and the tip of his tail curled in greeting, then he went back to sleep.

I leaned over the playpen to stroke Holly's hair. She was sucking on her fist, deep in dreamland with no idea that her mother was about to abandon her.

Get a grip, Kyra. Leaving for a few days on a job is not abandonment. My brain spoke logic. My heart didn't. I wanted to scoop her and hug her close. Instead, I leaned against Mason's desk. He finished typing a message and looked up at me with a smile.

"You're home early." He opened my hand and placed a kiss on my palm. The touch of his lips on that sensitive skin sent a zing of desire right to my girl parts. He lingered over it, looking up at me with dark mischief in his eyes, and I wondered why I ever left this house for anything. Then I remembered. A girl can't live by kisses alone, though it would be fun to try.

"I…uh…have some news." I pulled my hand away before I forgot myself and yanked him into the bedroom.

He quirked an eyebrow at me.

"I got a job offer from Roden and Hogg Reclamation Services. Have you heard of them?"

"Sure. They're big into industrial scavenging. So big, they have several ministers in their back pocket."

I showed him the contract and explained the job.

"I wasn't sure I should take it. This close to Christmas and everything."

"But you did." His brows were furrowed.

"I did. It's really good money."

Here it comes. He won't want me taking off on my own.

"It's not about the money." His lips were pressed flat. He didn't want me to go.

The rant I'd been holding in all the way home burst from me.

"So just because I have a baby, I should stay home and give up any chance of furthering my business? This job is important. It's more than a reference on my resumé. It will open doors for Valkyrie Pest Control. It means…"

"Whoa! Rein it in!" Mason held up his hands in surrender. "I didn't mean you shouldn't go. Of course you should go! I'd go with you, if I could. All I want is for you to be safe. R&H has a good reputation and a private militia. I want to know that they guarantee your safety."

"Oh." That was it? His whole argument was that he didn't want me to get killed? I couldn't really disagree with that. "Carmen—she's the one who hired me—has assured me that we'll be well protected." Of course, there were no real assurances when it came to the Inbetween and we both knew it.

Mason ran a hand through his hair, making it stick up at the back. I called it his mad scientist look. Out in public, he was always well-groomed. The mad scientist was all mine. I let my fingers roam through the curls.

"I know it's close to Christmas, but we'll be back in plenty of time to trim the tree."

"Don't worry about that. If you have to go, this is a good time. The parliament is out of session until the New Year. I can be home most days with Holly."

"Really? That would put my mind at ease, knowing you're here."

"I'll be here." He smiled and tugged me down on his lap. "I'll miss you though." He kissed my neck and his lips edged their way down to the V of my shirt. Only one button was open, but he deftly undid another to get at bare skin.

I was just wondering if we could sneak away while the baby was sleeping when the back door by the kitchen opened and slammed shut again. A wet hell hound bounded into the room to snuffle Grim's butt. The night-jaguar hissed and batted at Princess before taking off in a puffed-up huff. Behind Princess came the voices of Raven and Jacoby raised in a quarrel.

I sighed and stood up. Afternoon nookie was over-rated anyway.

"You were off-side!" Raven shouted. "The goal didn't count!"

"Offs side? I ons side!" Jacoby shouted back.

We'd installed an ice rink for the boys a few weeks back, and I'd taught them to play hockey to keep them busy until soccer season started again. Unfortunately, Raven and the goblits never saw eye-to-eye in any sports arena. And now it sounded like they'd dragged Jacoby into their feud.

"Off side!"

"Ons side!" The shouting escalated…aaand now the baby was awake and crying. I picked her up and jiggled her on my hip. The sound of her cries immediately made my milk turn on like I was a spigot.

"I'll feed her," I said to Mason. "You sort out those two knuckleheads before they start brawling in the kitchen."

"Gladly." Mason put on his fatherly frown and went into the kitchen. I took my baby to the bedroom and settled on the divan to nurse. One of her little fists clasped onto the edge of my open shirt. The other pressed against my bare skin. Her eyes were closed, blond lashes sweeping against her cheek. She looked like an angel, and I wondered how I was ever going to leave her.

CHAPTER

5

The Inbetween encompassed all the land left after civilization moved into protected wards. During the Flood Wars, bombs of pure magic were dropped like candy over cities and suburbs. First, they were meant to subdue populations. By the end of the war, the bombs were an attempt to stave off the demons that came through the cracks in the veil—cracks formed from the first bombs.

In hindsight, it all seems ridiculous, a little like cutting off your head to cure brain cancer. But hindsight is as clear as a crystal ball and just about as helpful.

All this excess magic laying around meant that I had no idea how to pack for a December excursion into the Inbetween. The weather would be unpredictable and the terrain could be anything from swamp to icy mountains. I tried to pack light, but I needed my winter camping gear, thermal boots, extra gloves and hat and my down jacket. If we passed through a rogue puddle of magic that suddenly caused summer to appear, I could peel off a few layers. Better to be too warm than too cold.

For weapons, I took only my sword and my hunting knife. Carmen said we'd ride with a full complement of militia guards. They'd have the fire power.

I was debating which pair of wool socks to add to the pack and ended up jamming in both pairs, when I noticed Jacoby outside my bedroom door. He hung on the door jamb with one finger in his mouth like a toddler. The other hand tugged at the work belt slung over his shoulder like a bandoleer.

I sighed and zipped my bag shut. I'd known this confrontation was coming.

"You can come in," I said.

Jacoby startled, then sashayed in like he hadn't been waiting to catch my attention.

I checked the pockets on my bag, making sure all my small items were secured. Jacoby hung onto the bed frame, swaying side to side. Nope, nothing to see here.

"You have something you want to tell me?" I asked.

He gave in and slumped on the bed in a pile of furry arms and legs.

"Kyra-lady promises never to do it again." He pouted.

"Do what?" I knew exactly what.

"To leaves me."

I looked into his big coppery-brown eyes. They were puddled with tears.

Oh, boy. Last year I had made an emergency trip to Asgard to save my pregnancy. When I left, I assumed it was a one way trip, with no chance of coming home. The thought of it still tugged my heart into my throat. I'd taken Raven and Princess—Raven because he was my responsibility and Princess because she went where Raven went. I'd left everyone else behind, even Mason. I'd foolishly believed that Jacoby would be happier here in his new home with his new family. I'd been wrong. We'd made up since then, but clearly he still had abandonment issues.

"I'm not leaving you." I dropped my bag on the floor and scooped him into my lap. Jacoby and I had an an odd relationship. It wasn't lovey-dovey, full of kisses and cuddles. He wasn't a puppy. But I got a hug once in a while, when one of us really needed it. Jacoby needed it now. I kissed the top of his head. It smelled like campfire embers. I smoothed down his hair that curled like poodle fur.

"I'll be home in a few days. I promise. Then we'll celebrate Christmas just like we planned."

"But I's your 'prentice," he said almost too softly to hear.

"You are, but even apprentices get time off. In fact, by law you get two weeks paid vacation."

"Paid? I's paid?"

"Of course you are. I set up an account in your name. I've been depositing money into it every two weeks."

It was true. I was going to tell him at the Yule celebration. Second class fae could only get bank accounts if they were co-signed by a ward citizen. Brownies and gnomes were terrible with money. Give them a few coins and they inevitably spent it on drink and food, so mostly they never had a reason to save.

Jacoby's eyes shone like enormous Christmas balls. "A bank? I has a bank?"

"A bank account," I corrected. "And savings. When I get home I'll teach you how to access your money, okay?"

"Yes!"

"In the mean time, you have two whole weeks off. You can do whatever you want to do."

He rubbed a furry fist over his furry face.

"I wants to go with Kyra-lady."

His little fist might as well have squeezed my heart dry.

"Not this time. You should stay home and enjoy your time off." I wasn't going to make excuses, but I didn't want to expose Jacoby to the dangers of the Inbetween. "Besides, baby Holly loves you. She'll be sad if we both go." His expression brightened.

"I helps baby play while Kyra-lady's gone?"

"That would be a big help. That's exactly what families do." He nodded sagely like he'd known this all along. I patted him on the head and he scampered away.

The next goodbyes would be harder.

An hour later, my bags were packed and I was ready to leave. I peeked into Raven's room.

"I'm going now," I said from the doorway. He glanced up from his widget and gave me a "'K," before turning back to whatever fascinating game he'd been playing. For a kid who'd grown up without the Ley-net, he'd sure learned the pleasures of the digital world quickly.

I crossed the room to his bed, dropped a kiss on his forehead, and smoothed back his hair. He accepted the ministrations with a small smile. I wanted to give him some last instructions, like to pick up after Princess or to stay out of fights with the twins, but just in case the worst happened, I didn't want those to be the last words he remembered from me.

"Love you," I said.

For a brief moment, his thumbs paused in their mad attempt to shoot space lasers. He looked up. "You too."

I would take it. Coming from a thirteen-year-old, it was as close to a declaration of filial love as I would get.

My next stop was the barn. It was the post-breakfast, pre-lunch lull and most of the critters were asleep. That was fine. I'd already said my goodbyes the night before. I was here just for Kur.

He was curled in a white fluffy ball at the back of his cage. I ran my fingers through his downy fur, and he blinked big eyes at me.

"Hey, buddy. Want to go on an adventure?"

He chirped softly.

"That's right. It's cold and snowy outside. Just how you like it." I scooped him up and he climbed up my arm to rest on my shoulder. I could feel him vibrating through my jacket. Ice sprites didn't exactly purr, but when he was excited he quivered and hummed like a bumblebee.

Yes, an adventure was just what the doctor ordered for a down-in-the-dumps ice sprite.

Mason waited outside with Holly bundled in her snowsuit and tucked into a sled with blankets.

"I thought it would be a good distraction for me and the Poupoune to go for a walk so we don't have to watch you leave." In old French, a *poupoune* was a swaddled baby, and it had become one of Mason's pet names for Holly. His eyes were dark gray like a thunderous ridge of storm clouds. The Poupoune watched me with those same eyes.

I couldn't help it. A sob burst from my throat. I snatched her up, blankets and all and squeezed. This bizarre behavior from Mom elicited a yelp and then a full blown wail. I smothered her damp cheeks in kisses. She fussed until Kur head-butted her and she cooed. I handed her over to Mason and wiped my eyes.

"Go for your walk. You're right. I won't be able to leave with you standing here."

Mason tucked Holly back into her sled, then pulled me into a hug.

"It's only a few days."

There were two jackets and two shirts between us, but I could keen the beat of his heart, slow and tolling like a church bell, and now a little clouded with the dark magic he'd inherited in the Nether. His magic was like his scent, unique and unmistakeable. I wished I could bottle it and take some with me.

Kur grabbed Mason's chin with his tiny human-like hands and made a trilling sound.

I know exactly how you feel, I thought.

"Is he going with you?" Mason grinned and rubbed Kur behind an ear.

"Yeah. It seemed like a good idea."

Mason nodded. Then his eyes turned serious, and I tucked the ice sprite under my arm. Mason's lips found mine and he kissed me, not like a goodbye but like a promise of what was to come when I came home.

"Miss you already," I said.

"Miss you more." He kissed me again, then took the handle of the sled. I watched my family trundle off into the snow. Kur squirmed to be let go. With a frozen heart, I headed for my van.

Forty minutes later, I parked in a garage under the R&H headquarters in the north end of the city and transferred my bag to Carmen's sleek black sedan.

"We're taking this into the Inbetween?" I eyed the car skeptically. The tires looked like solid winter tires, but they wouldn't get us far once the roads disappeared.

Carmen smiled. She was dressed in black and gray military fatigues that still managed to look stylish on her tall form.

"No. We'll be meeting my crew in Barrows and leaving the car there. I hope you packed for a hike."

"This isn't my first Inbetween rodeo." I smiled back at her.

"Of course not. That's why I hired you."

I wasn't sure what to make of Carmen. Animals were more my thing. Reading people always felt like deciphering a code without the super-secret decoder ring. Avalon was my only true female friend and she—

"Hey ladies! All ready for our girls' weekend out?" Avie called from the exit of the garage. She lugged a huge suitcase on wheels and another pack on her back. She was dressed in a style that could only be called hedge-witch on ice. She even had a pair of skates hanging by their laces over one shoulder.

Carmen watched her approach with her arms crossed and lips pressed flat. "I told you to pack light."

"You also told me to pack for any emergency." Avie yanked her suitcase upright and slumped onto it.

"So what emergency would require ice skates?" Carmen said.

"I don't know. An ice emergency? It's winter after all. Hey, Kyra. I bet you're surprised to see me."

"Little bit."

"I decided I earned a few days away from the kids, so I asked to tag along."

"To the Inbetween?"

"Uh-huh." Avie was fishing in her backpack for something and not really paying attention.

"You realize people die in the Inbetween?"

"Uh-huh."

I grabbed her elbow and shook it.

"Avie, seriously. What are you doing here?"

She abandoned whatever she'd been looking for and turned to face me. Her eyes were glassy and she bit her bottom lip to hold back tears.

"Trevor and I had a fight."

"You guys never fight." I didn't know how they did it with nine kids, but they always seemed like the picture-perfect family.

"Well, we did. And it was nasty. We both decided that I should spend some time away."

I rounded on Carmen. "And you agreed to this?"

"What are friends for?" When Carmen saw the outrage on my face, she changed tactics. "Don't look so serious. We'll be perfectly safe. You'll see. We'll caravan with the militia, staying in Hub's safe camps along the way. The bulla is about fifty clicks west of Annequin Lodge. Avie will wait for us there. She can have a massage or something."

"Sounds perfect." Avie sighed.

I'd been to Annequin lodge. They didn't offer massages. The only form of entertainment was watching the fire burn down in the hearth in the main hall.

"Kyra, stop frowning," Avie said. "You're making me feel unwelcome." She was biting her lip again.

"Of course you're welcome." In fact, I would appreciate the buffer between me and Carmen. "I just don't think it's safe."

"Oh, come on. You get to have the big adventures all the time. It's my turn."

"And an adventure it will be," Carmen said. "But we'll have to get you kitted up properly once we're in Barrows."

I gave in and helped Avie load her monstrous suitcase into the car.

THE BULLA LAY north of Montreal Ward in what used to be an industrial park near what used to be the town of Morin Heights. Now thick forest covered the town, and the industrial park was a magic wasteland.

All this Carmen explained as we drove over Crystal Bridge and out the north gate. The R&H caravan was waiting for us in Barrows, the shanty town at the base of the gate. Here, homesteaders came to trade, refugees sought visas into the ward, and predators preyed on the weak and desperate.

I thought we'd meet the others at one of Barrows' many inns, but Carmen pulled up to a gated compound on the northern edge of town. Beyond the compound lay nothing but snow frosted trees. Two armed guards nodded at her as they opened the gate and stood with guns pointed into the forest as it closed behind us.

"Your bags will be transferred to the caravan. Go ahead inside." Carmen pointed to a cement bunker-like building. "There's refreshments. I have a few things to check on. We leave in an hour."

"Aye-aye, Captain," Avie saluted.

Carmen flipped her the finger. "Just behave around my soldiers. They're not used to civilians."

Kur had fallen asleep on the drive. I shook him awake and he settled on my shoulder like an owl on a branch. Avie grabbed my hand and tugged me toward the building.

"Isn't this going to be fun?" She seemed to have put aside her upset over the fight with Trevor and was determined to keep up with the charade that we were a couple of gals out on the town.

"Sure. It'll be smashing. You might even call it killer."

"Oh, Kyra, don't be such a party pooper. Carmen says we'll be safe and I trust her."

"How long have you two known each other?"

"Since I stole her purple crayon and she stabbed me with her scissors. They were safety scissors, but still—ow! We bonded while sitting on the bench outside the principal's office. We were terrified we'd be kicked out of kindergarten."

"So a long time then." I chose a mug from a stack on a folding table and filled it with hot tea.

Avie grabbed a cookie and took a bite. "Yeah, but we lost touch after high school. Children give Carmen hives. I can't say I blame her. What was I thinking? Nine kids?" She groaned and shoved the rest of the cookie in her mouth. Kur chirped and tried to grab her cookie, so I gave him one. Several soldiers were openly watching us now, probably wondering what new kind of monster they were taking on.

"Nine kids, Kyra! Do you know what that's like? There's never any silence in my house. Never! Even when they're sleeping they make noise. Last night, in the middle of the night, I tripped over something on the way to the bathroom. I thought it was a toy—because you know those are everywhere—but no, it was Fiona, asleep on the tile floor. I didn't even know she how she got out of her crib. She probably had help. Her and Laraby are plotting to take over the world one day. I can see it...oh!" She saw the look on my face. "I'm sorry. You're still in that new mother phase, when they're all angels. I bet you think baby barf is cute."

I shrugged thinking of the spit up on Mason's shirt. It wasn't *not* cute.

Avie choked down another cookie. "Well, you just wait until they're fourteen and start drinking in the park before school dances. The barf isn't so cute then." She collapsed into a folding chair, a cookie in each hand. There were crumbs on her shirt.

I patted her shoulder. "Everything will be all right." By the gods, I was a terrible friend. What a platitude. *Everything will be all right.* How could I know that? Life is hard, sometimes brutal. The only real assurance I could give her was that we wouldn't get out of it alive.

But Avie grabbed onto the pathetic lifeline I'd thrown her.

"You think so?" Her big eyes stared up at me. Her lip, flecked with crumbs, trembled. I squeezed her shoulder again.

"I'm sure of it. Everyone keeps telling me not to blink. That babies grow up so fast. So it must be true, right? This won't last forever. And by the time you get home, Trevor will be so glad you're back. You'll sort it out. You'll see." A new thought occurred to me. "Did you tell him where you're going?"

Avie's eyes shifted back to the cookie plate. "Not exactly. He just knows we're going to an inn. I didn't want to worry him."

That was probably a good idea. Now I just had to keep her alive until we returned so I wouldn't have to look Trevor in the eye and explain that I'd let dragons eat his wife.

CHAPTER

6

The caravan consisted of six trucks, led by two troop transports that carried six soldiers each. Our van came next, and the supply truck followed us with two more transport trucks behind that. Truck wasn't exactly the right word though. I'd never seen vehicles quite like these. They were part SUV and part tank. Each transport had a gun tower on the roof.

Our van was also armored, but without the gun turret. I sat in the front seat beside Carmen. Avie was already asleep in the back. I thought, more than anything, she probably just needed rest. Poor kid.

Kur was already worn out from all the sights and had curled up in the crook of Avie's belly to sleep.

As soon as we left the relative ease of Barrows, the caravan train came to a snow-crunching halt.

"We're stopping already?" I asked. We hadn't been on the road for half an hour.

"Don't bother getting out," Carmen said. "We're just swapping out the tires."

Carmen flicked a switch on the dash and the truck rose slowly as if someone were cranking a hydraulic jack under it. I watched through the windshield as soldiers hopped out of the transports. Two rushed to our van while the others took care of their own. Wheels folded under the trucks and out of sight. From long, narrow trunks along the sides, the soldiers pulled out fat skis and fitted them to the chassis up front. Where the back tires had been, a row of belted wheels now clicked into place.

A soldier pounded a fist on Carmen's window to let us know they were done, and she flicked the switch to ease the truck down onto the snow. The whole procedure took less than ten minutes, and we were on our way again.

"Fancy," I said.

"Only the best," Carmen said. "We should be at Annequin Lodge tomorrow by midmorning."

"Assuming we don't get waylaid by marauders or a herd of angry bison. Or a swarm of killer wasps."

"Don't be silly. There are no wasps in December." Carmen flashed me a smile. "Look in there." She pointed to the console between our seats. "I couldn't get enough for all the troops, but there's no reason for us to do without."

I lifted the console cover to find a thermos and three metal mugs. Opening the thermos filled the car with the exquisite scent of coffee.

"Dear Odin All-father. I have never smelled anything so good." I hadn't had coffee in weeks.

I poured two mugs. There was no sugar or creamer, but I didn't care. I fitted a mug into the cup holder for Carmen and wrapped my hands around another.

"Yeah, those godlings are a real pain in the ass," she said.

Montreal fed its populace from greenhouses all along its southern frontier. Hub militia guarded these farms like the precious resources they were. Mostly, they were vigilant about threats from the outside—wild animals, marauders and desperate homesteaders. They hadn't figured on an attack coming from their own citizens.

The godlings, a small group of humans who could trace their bloodlines back to the gods of various pantheons, wanted to form their own political party in Montreal. Right now, they had the choice to vote with the fae, humans or alchemists. The godlings felt none of these gave them a voice in parliament.

Their protests had started as rallies and publicity stunts, like when the Olympians had highjacked Mason's official bid for Prime Minister last year. Only the animosity between the pantheons kept the revolt in disarray, but I'd heard rumors that the various godling leaders were in truce talks. If they ever made peace among themselves, it would be messy for the rest of us.

Last year, they'd blown up an apex tower and rail road tracks, delaying the union between Montreal and Manhattan. In the spring, they'd targeted a sector of Montreal's greenhouses. It so happened that the sector they chose housed mostly coffee and kale plants. No one much missed the kale. But coffee rations had sparked more riots within the city.

"I understand where they're coming from," I said. Though I voted with the alchemists, I was technically a godling too. And the whole taxation without representation thing rankled a bit. "But I wish they would find some other way to protest. Coffee should be sacrosanct."

"Amen." Carmen lifted her mug.

So far, we'd been following an old highway and though the snow was deep, it was fairly clear of obstructions. Carmen had let the truck drive itself, but now we turned off the highway, and she switched over to manual control.

Snow was falling in those fat, sluggish flakes that look so picturesque on holiday cards. Until the flakes grew as big as dinner plates. Each one hit the windshield with a splat. The wipers couldn't keep up. The radio crackled with reports from other trucks.

"Do we stop? Advise." I recognized the voice of Richard Kierklo, the captain of R&H's militia. I'd met him in Barrows before we left.

Carmen tapped a button on the console and spoke into a mic hidden somewhere in the truck. "Negative. It's an anomaly. Push on."

My spidey sense was tingling. The Inbetween could throw out nasty weather phenomena, but this felt like more than that. I keened a growing power around us, not a surge so much as a pooling of magic. I'd experienced this before. Mason and I nearly got trapped in a pool once. It had almost forced him to turn gargoyle.

"We need to move faster," I said.

"We can't." Carmen's knuckles were white on the steering wheel. "I can't see a thing."

I gripped the handhold above my head as our truck hit a bump and was airborne for a second. It landed with a bone-jarring thud.

"What's going on?" Avie said in a groggy voice. Her head poked between the front seats. "What the hells is that?"

"Snow," I said. The magic was brewing around us now, percolating like a coffee pot on over-boil.

"Are any of your soldiers shifters?" I asked.

Carmen shot me a frown. "Two. Arnaut and Dagg."

"You've got to stop now!"

The truck in front of us stopped so suddenly, we almost drove into it. Carmen hit the brakes and we skidded sideways.

She jabbed the console. "Report."

Raised voices came over the radio. The snarl of an angry wolf. More shouting. Silence.

"Kierklo, report!"

Static crackled, then came Kierklo's ragged voice. "Dagg shifted, but he's sedated now. No injuries. McCabe report."

Another voice came on, one I didn't recognize but assumed to be from another transport. "Wellman was bitten, but it's a minor wound. Arnaut is sedated. All clear."

"All clear," repeated Kierklo.

All clear until the next full moon, when poor Wellman would have to be locked up until it was determined if he'd turn into a werewolf. Normally, the infection rate from a minor bite was infinitesimal, but with the Inbetween's magic at play, all bets were off.

Carmen relaxed into her seat and shot me a wry glance. "This isn't our first trip into the abyss. We have protocols for these situations. Though it would be handy to know about them ahead of time. How'd you do that?"

"I have a sensitivity to magic." I left it at that. Just because Carmen was paying me a boatload of money didn't mean she had the right to all my secrets. And I magnanimously didn't remind her that I *had* warned her.

"Is that coffee I smell?" Avie asked. I poured a mug and handed it back to her.

"Mmm." She stuck her nose deep into the rising steam. "So, what's going on?"

"We hit a hot spot," Carmen said. "No need to worry. We'll be out of it soon."

The caravan rolled on again. My skin itched until we reached the edge of the magic pool, then I sank back in my seat. My shoulders ached from tensing.

"Better?" Carmen shot me a glance.

"Yeah, we're out of it."

Kur jumped from the back seat. His wings fluttered as he landed in my lap. The claws on his back feet pricked my leg as he tried to peer out the window. He chirped at the falling snow and pressed his face to the glass.

"You can't go out there yet, but soon." I ran my hand down his back. How could something be so fluffy and so sleek at the same time? The feel of his fur and the soft vibrations of a happy ice sprite calmed me.

We drove for over an hour in that blinding snow. I don't know how Carmen did it. The flakes thrashed against the windshield. It was mesmerizing and disorienting, but Carmen seemed relaxed. She tapped the steering wheel with one finger as if she listened to some rhythm that the rest of us couldn't hear.

The snow came to an end in that whimsical way of the Inbetween, and I don't mean it just stopped falling from the sky. Our skis suddenly ground against dirt as we drove from a blizzard into a green, summery glade.

"Convert," Kierklo said over the radio, and once again the soldiers emerged to change skis for tires.

"They might be changing those back in five minutes," I said.

"Then they'll change them." Carmen's tone wasn't snappish. She was resigned.

Green grass rolled under our tires. I craned my neck to look out the rear window. Behind us, a wall of white rose like a curtain. These little pockets of contrary seasons weren't uncommon in the Inbetween.

The interior of the truck became warm, then hot. Kur started to pant.

"Where's the button to roll down the window," Avie asked.

"No windows." Carmen cranked the air conditioner.

"I can't even feel that back here," Avie whined.

Carmen shot me a glance and shook her head as if to say, *civilians.*

"It's not a good idea to open the windows," I told Avie. "See those bugs?"

"Are they dangerous?" Avie peered out the window at a cloud of gnats hovering above the road.

"Could be," Carmen said. "We're not going to find out."

The gnats coalesced into a cloud and swarmed the truck. They battered against the windshield. Carmen turned on the wipers, but they just smeared the mess over the glass. She slowed until she could see through the muck.

Ahead of us, the transport was nearly lost in the miasma of insects.

Carmen hit the console radio again. "All units, hostile protocol one. Repeat, hostile protocol one." She flicked another switch. "This seals the truck. All our air is being recycled and filtered for now. Nothing bigger than a freckle on a microbe's ass can get through." She hit another switch and screens dropped over the windows. We were navigating solely by cameras and sensors now. The windshield lit up, turning into a giant high resolution screen that would make my favorite alchemist inventor, Oscar Lewis, wet his pants.

I was impressed. For the first time on this trip I felt, if not safe, at least well-protected.

Outside, rain started to fall. The gnats dispersed. The land was flat and treeless, but covered in thigh-high ferns. Our trucks easily rolled over them. The light was gray and foreboding. Carmen played with the dashboard controls and smaller screens opened within the bigger windshield screen. These showed the views above, behind and on either side. Dark clouds seethed overhead.

Kur squealed and pawed at the window. I tucked him into my jacket and made soothing noises. His tiny claws raked the flesh under my shirt, but the confinement settled him.

We drove toward a black wall of mountains that spread to the horizon on either side.

"Is this on your map?" I asked. It didn't seem likely that Carmen would take us by an impassible route.

"The mountains yes. But last time we came this way, this anomaly wasn't here."

So the freak summer weather was new.

"And what about that?" I pointed to a pillar of white looming ahead.

"Not that either. Any idea what it is?"

"No."

It looked like a giant column of marble, but it seemed to be moving. Maybe the gnats were swarming it? We were too far away to get a good read on its magic, but as we drew closer, I didn't need my keening to know it was bad. Really bad.

"We have to turn around," I said. Kur whined inside my jacket.

A burst of static and chatter came from the radio. The soldiers had seen it too. The column wasn't marble, and it wasn't surrounded by gnats.

It was a vortex—spinning, eating up ground, whipping up dirt, leaves and branches. And growing.

"Gyrus!" someone shouted over the radio.

"Oh, shit." Carmen punched a button on the console, bringing up a map. She scanned the terrain, looking for a way around.

A gyrus spun and writhed like a tornado, but it was really a portal. Get sucked inside and you could be spit out anywhere on Terra. That's if you made it through. According to the rare gyrus survivors, the trip was like riding in a giant washing machine on overdrive.

Carmen switched off the map. "Can't turn around. The only way through those mountains is on the other side of that thing."

The gyrus had been traveling slowly across our path. Now it changed angles and, like a crocodile suddenly spotting a duck, it began creeping toward us.

"Disband!" Carmen shouted. The trucks turned away from the convoy line, driving in all different directions.

The gyrus suddenly sped forward, then swerved to cut us off. Carmen jerked the wheel hard right and we lurched over a tuft of grass. The van's engine screamed. Console lights blinked and the screens went out for a second. The truck skimmed the outer edge of the gyrus. It hit us like a slap from an angry titan, and we spun.

Avie screamed.

Kur gouged my flesh with his claws.

Carmen cursed.

And I hung on to my seat as the world careened around us.

We came to a stop with a bone-jarring thump. We were blind while the cameras rebooted. Carmen frantically pushed buttons. She called up curses to multiple gods as the engine stuttered and complained.

A sound like thunder rumbled over the clearing. The gyrus had turned to make another pass at us.

Screams blasted through the radio. Men and women shouted orders, curses and prayers.

Our cameras came back online just in time for us to witness the vortex swallowing a transport. Metal and glass sheared away from it, blasting another truck like shrapnel. Thunder roared again and the gyrus rolled over the second truck, swallowing it in seconds. Screams of pain and anger turned to shrieks of fear and then nothing but crackling silence.

Ahead, I could see the pass through the mountains. It seemed impossibly small.

Carmen's swearing finally got the engine started. She forced the van to give everything it had. We bounced over ferns and bushes, not bothering to look for the route of least resistance, until we hit dirt. The tires skidded. We hurtled through the pass, and spun to a stop. Another truck pulled up beside us. The supply truck was next, and then another transport.

We waited. Nothing. Of the six trucks, only four had made it past the gyrus.

And snow began to fall from the darkening sky.

BUCKLE IN FOR A WILD RIDE: GYRUSES

July 3, 2070

Let's talk about the weather. I know, when I started this blog over a month ago, I promised fascinating insights into all creatures wild and woolly—not small talk about the weather. But hear me out.

What if weather can be sentient?

Sounds crazy, doesn't it? But I believe that's exactly what I experienced last month. Some of you might have seen my posts about draikas and rock-skippers. During that same trip, I came across an unusual weather phenomenon. My guide called it a gyrus and warned me not to get in its way.

The gyrus looked like a small dust devil, a mini tornado of dirt and debris marching across the countryside like a tumble weed. Not too scary, right? I thought so too, until my guide warned me that stepping into the gyrus was like stepping into a portal. "A portal to where?" I asked.

Anywhere. On Terra or another world. Yikes! That's not a trip I want to make. Not ever!

Tornados, even small ones, are terrifying because of their random destructiveness. You can't argue with a force of nature, can't plead with it to leave your home untouched, can't even try to deflect it. There is no point in asking why your house was destroyed and the neighbor's left untouched. That indifference is both frightening and somehow comforting. If a ghoul attacks your family, you hunt it and kill it. But if a tornado takes out your house, you have no outlet for vengeance. You simply pull up your socks and rebuild.

I mention all this because there was something…off about the gyrus. Its actions didn't feel random. It was stalking us. And I swear, I could sense a consciousness swirling in all that debris.

So what if a gyrus is more than a freak of nature? What if it's a sentient creature, and its victims aren't actually transported, but eaten?

Like I said. Crazy. But indulge me. I'd like to understand this phenomenon more, before I encounter another one. Can anyone confirm that they or someone they know have survived going through a gyrus?

COMMENTS (4)

I can confirm it. My brother stumbled into a gyrus. It took him halfway across the continent and left him unconscious in the middle of a frozen desert. It took him 4 years to get home.
CampCay1 (July 18, 2070)

———•———

My daughter was taken by a gyrus. We never saw her again.
Hula556 (August 4, 2070)

———•———

Maybe the act of transporting people is how it eats? Like the portal is a digestive tract, of sorts?
cchedgewitch (August 5, 2070)

>   That's a really interesting theory.
>   *Valkyrie367 (August 5, 2070)*

s soon as I let him out of the van, Kur tumbled in the snow, then shot upward. His wings fluttered. He landed on a pine bough, knocked the snow off it in a cascade and chirped happily. I knew he wouldn't go far, so I let him be and turned my attention to the camp.

When Mason and I journeyed to Annequin Lodge, it had been a three-day trek. Of course we rode Wild Hunt beasts, not super sleek trucks on skis. This time, we could have made it in one day, if we'd driven through the night, but no one wanted to brave the dubious roads of the Inbetween in the dark.

The camp was provided by Hub for use by travelers. It was little more than a cement bunker with a secure door and chimney. From my past experience, I knew the bunker would be stocked with food for humans and mounts. There would be wood for a fire and a couple of beds too.

Carmen gave the order to make camp and the trucks circled the bunker, their headlights pointing into the dark forest.

"I'm going to let the wounded have the bunks," Carmen said. "You ladies don't mind camping in the rough, do you?"

Avie grumbled, but I didn't mind. Carmen's concern for her soldiers shone a new light on her. She'd handled the blows the Inbetween threw at her with professional calm and confidence. Her people respected her and followed her commands without question.

According to the reports, one transport had been shredded in the outer edge of the gyrus. They'd rescued only one soldier from that wreckage. Her leg was broken and she had a gash on her head.

The other transport had been sucked right into the vortex. Nothing remained.

Captain Kierklo had been among those lost, so Lieutenant McCabe reported the losses and injuries to Carmen. She listened with a flat expression. When he was done, she said, "Let the wounded have the bunks inside. Set up shelters for the rest."

McCabe nodded and turned to the others who were already digging through snowdrifts to reach the door.

Carmen's lips pinched in a hard line as she watched them. I got the feeling she was counting to ten to control her rage.

"It's possible that Kierklo and the others will come out somewhere else," I said. She nodded. "Somewhere nearby, hopefully." But we both knew that the portal could have opened anywhere on Terra or even into another dimension.

"My people are trained for such eventualities," she said. "If they're alive, they'll find a way home."

Nothing more was said of the incident as we all turned to the task of making camp.

I found a shovel in the trunk of our van and lent a hand to digging out the bunker. As soon as the door was clear, the soldier with the broken leg and Wellman, who'd been bitten by the werewolf, were brought inside. Arnaut who'd shifted during the magic overload was examined by the medic and deemed fit for service again. Dagg, the second shifter, had been in the missing transport along with Captain Kierklo and his team.

Of the twenty-two soldiers who'd left with our caravan, only thirteen remained, and two of those were injured. The others set a perimeter watch, cleared snow and built fires with the efficiency of a group who'd worked together for many years. A dark-haired woman handed me three ration packs. I wondered what was going through her head. Had she been close to the missing soldiers? Was death just part of the job? I thanked her for the food and she nodded, giving away nothing.

Once a perimeter was established, the transport headlights were turned off to preserve the night vision of those on watch. The camp suddenly seemed utterly dark, like those disorienting moments right upon waking after a bad dream. But three fires crackled in the icy clearing and my vision soon adjusted to their soft light.

Carmen set her bedroll beside one fire and I joined her. Avie was already bundled in her parka and a blanket, staring into the flames. The soldiers split up around the remaining two fires, eating and chatting in low voices.

I laid down a tarp and unrolled my sleeping bag, glad that I'd splurged on the bed warmer. The ground was hard and lumpy. I smoothed it out and something squirmed under my bedding. I flipped back the tarp and found a tiny, glassy stone…with legs.

"Ack!" Avie let out a yelp and scrambled away. "What is that?"

I held up the tiny beast. It had a transparent shell that displayed its organs pumping away inside.

"I don't know, ice turtle, maybe?" I'd never seen anything like it. Four stumpy legs waggled as I held it in the air. A round head with a sharp curving beak strained to twist and bite my hand.

"Aw, look. It's trying to eat you," Avie said.

"Adorable." I set the strange little reptile aside. It sat frozen in fear for a moment, then it trundled off into the snowbank. I scanned the ground for more living ice lumps.

"Not sure I want more of those sneaking into my bedroll tonight."

Avie made a face and crossed her arms over her chest. "I think I'll sleep in the truck."

"Come on," Carmen said. "Where's your sense of adventure?"

"I think it's frozen along with my feet." She rubbed her arms and stamped her feet.

"Don't worry. I got you a state-of-the-art bedroll. You'll be snug as a bug."

Avie didn't look convinced. Mentioning bugs probably wasn't a great idea. Her eyes looked into the darkness between the trees.

"What else is out there?"

"Do you really want to know?" Carmen asked.

Avie hugged her blanket more tightly around her.

"No."

Supper was melted snow and dry rations. Avie read off the ingredients on her ration pack. "This isn't bad stuff. I wouldn't mind it for a quick supper during the week."

I had choked down my rations—a mix of nuts, oats and dried veggies—with big gulps of water.

"You know what this needs?" Carmen rifled through her pack and came out with a metal water bottle. She unscrewed it, took a swig and passed it to me. It smelled like wine, but when I sipped, it burned down the back of my throat. I coughed as I passed the bottled to Avie.

"Smooth." My eyes were watering.

"I don't remember the last time I had wine on a school night." Avie sipped and passed it back to Carmen.

Carmen saluted her with the bottle. "Wine any time is one of the great things about living alone."

"Oh, gods," Avie groaned. "I miss living alone. Don't you, Kyra?"

"Not really." I hadn't been cohabitating long enough to miss the lonely nights from my previous years.

"There are just some things you can't do with a man around," Avie said.

"Like what?"

"Like put on your favorite jeans from high school even if they don't fit and eat peanut butter right from the jar while listening to emo bands at top volume until you start crying."

For a moment, only the crackle of the fire responded, then Carmen said, "That was oddly specific."

Avie chugged down another swig of the fortified wine and wiped a drip from her lips on her sleeve.

Carmen took the bottle. "I get it though. I need my alone time."

Avie snorted. "You just don't like kids."

"Damn right. Who needs all that snot?"

Avie nodded. "There is a lot of mucus. No one warns you about that, you know. You expect the poop and even the spit up. But not the snot."

I was feeling a little tipsy. And all the talk of babies made me homesick for little Holly, snot or no snot. Suddenly, I felt a warm gush down my stomach.

"Oh, shit." I rummaged in my bag and pulled out my breast pump.

"What is that?" Carmen asked.

"I'm, um…"

"She's leaking," Avie said with a knowing nod. "Sucks doesn't it?" She tossed back another sip of wine.

"I'll just be a minute." With my back turned to the soldiers' fires, I slipped the breast pumps under my shirt and set them pumping. Carmen looked on with an expression halfway between fascination and horror.

"It's a milking machine!"

"I bet that feels good," Avie said. "You have no idea what the pressure of a full boob is like."

She was right. The release was immediate and satisfying. I sat back with a sigh. My shirt was soaked, and I'd have to change it before I got chilled, but for now, the fire warmed me enough for comfort.

Carmen shook her head. "I don't know how you do it. Snot and pressurized milk and poop and all that screaming."

"Don't forget the stretch marks." Avie said. "And we won't even talk about the episiotomy scar."

Carmen looked at me. "Do I want to know what that is?"

I shook my head. "You really don't."

Avie handed the bottle back to Carmen. "And that's just getting them through babyhood. Wait until the little buggers learn to speak. You know what Fiona said to the check out clerk at the grocery store last week? Oh, the clerk thought she was so adorable with her little curls and chubby cheeks, then Fiona blurts out, "We wanted to go to the park today, but we couldn't because of the fucking rain."

Carmen snorted and choked on the wine.

"Sweet right?" Avie said. "That's what happens when you've got older siblings. They learn too fast. Mostly because the older ones never shut up. Once they learn to talk back, you're done for. Last week, I was in the middle of arguing with Gatsby about why you shouldn't lick other people's feet, when Bartie came out of the bathroom buck naked and dumped his dirty underwear on my kitchen table. There were skid marks in it! Kid's eleven years old and he can't wipe his own ass yet. But the best part was when he tried to explain why it wasn't his fault. They're all heathens." She stuffed a handful of rations in her mouth and looked at me for confirmation. I nodded, though I didn't really have anything bad to say about my teenager. Raven had lived rough for the first twelve years of his life, so maybe I expected less of him. He could be sullen and the fighting with the goblin twins was getting old, but all in all, he was a pretty good kid.

"Anyway, that's when I lost it. I started to yell and I just couldn't stop. Trevor came home in the middle of it and…and well, I guess I said some things I shouldn't have." Avie slouched as if she could disappear into her blanket.

48

I thought she'd say more, but her eyes were gazing inward now. I reached over and squeezed her arm.

"You guys will work it out," I said.

"I know." She shot me a shaky smile and wiped away a stray tear.

"Well, I'm glad to live alone." Carmen slapped her knee. "I have my little rituals that I'm not ready to give up for anyone."

"Oooh, tell me." Avie shook off her melancholy. She gripped Carmen's wrist and shook it. "Let me live vicariously."

Carmen got a twinkle in her eye. "Well, sometimes when I get home, I strip down to my underwear to make dinner."

"I bet they're lacy too, right? No granny panties."

Carmen looked aghast. "Never. Satin and lace only. Even under this horrible uniform. A girl's gotta keep some feminine secrets in her life."

"That's for sure," Avie said. "So what's next. Do you eat standing up by the kitchen sink? I used to do that before I had kids."

"Sometimes. But my real secret is that I don't cook."

"Never?" Avie's eyes were wide like Carmen was telling her a ghost story.

"Never. I order take out every night."

"I used to have popcorn for supper sometimes." I felt like I should contribute to the conversation. The wine was getting to me.

"Popcorn and wine. A great combination." Carmen held the bottle up in a salute.

"Then what?" Avie urged. "Tell me all the salacious details."

"Then nothing. I watch vids or read. Before bed, I do my nightly face wash ritual."

"How long does that take?"

"Not long. Half an hour tops. But good moisturizing is important."

"Half an hour?" Avie sighed. "If I get two minutes to pee in peace, I'm lucky. Usually I have at least three kids in the bathroom with me."

I nodded knowingly. "Princess likes to follow me into the bathroom."

"Is that your dog?" Carmen asked.

"Hell hound."

Carmen's eye brows rose. She looked at Avie. "She's kidding right?"

"Nope. She's got a banshee living with her too, and some kind of octopus. Oh, and a dervish thing that breathes fire."

"Jacoby doesn't breathe fire," I said. "He just smokes sometimes. And Hunter is a kraken, not an octopus."

Carmen whistled. "I knew you were the creature expert, but I didn't realize you took your work home with you."

"They're foster fails," I said. "Mostly I try to re-home the creatures I rescue, but sometimes that isn't possible."

"Like your little sprite friend?" Carmen asked. "What's his name again?"

"Kur." Where was he anyway? I hadn't seen him since we made camp.

The breast pump had taken the edge off. I plucked off the bottles and set them aside.

"What are you going to do with that milk?" Avie asked.

"What do you think? Make eggnog?" I said. "I'm going to dump it."

Avie stared at the trees again, looking thoughtful. "You know breast milk is excellent for creating a secure ward. Have you ever done it?"

I shook my head. I'd learned to make a pretty decent ward using my green magic, but a milk ward sounded intriguing. Or maybe that was the wine talking.

I ducked into the van to change out of my wet shirt. Avie waited for me with a shovel in hand.

"We'll have to dig down through the snow. It's best if the milk touches the earth directly." Her cheeks were flushed and she swayed a bit.

"Maybe stumbling around the camp after all that wine isn't such a good idea," I said.

"Don't be silly. I'm not even tipsy." She turned and stumbled over a hunk of ice, shot me a wry smile and headed toward the transport trucks.

The soldier on watch blocked our path.

"You can't go out there alone," she said.

"We're not going far." I pointed to the other side of the truck. "We're just going to set a ward around the camp."

The soldier nodded and told us to be quick.

Avie dug a hole in the snow.

"Sprinkle a bit of milk in there. Not too much," she said when I tipped the bottle into the hole. "We need to make it last, so we can circle the camp."

We trudged around the perimeter, digging holes and dribbling milk at intervals that coincided with the cardinal points. Each time, I sprinkled milk,

Avie invoked the goddess Terra to bless our offering. At the final stop, Avie glanced at the clear sky. The sickle moon had risen over the trees.

"A full moon would be better, but we'll make do. Now, since the sacrificial milk was yours, it would be better if you invoke the final blessing. Think you can do it?"

"I guess." Terra and I weren't really on speaking terms. I thought of those few times I'd witnessed her primeval self in my dreams. She hadn't seemed friendly.

"Good," Avie said. "Just center yourself and call for Terra to accept your sacrifice. That should link the ward together."

I sat cross-legged on the snow and closed my eyes. Angus and Errol had both trained me in the art of meditation and it was usually easy to drop into that calm space. But tonight, it wouldn't come.

Where was Kur anyway?

A rumbling sound filled the night. I snuck a peek at the sky. It wasn't unheard of to get thunderstorms in the Inbetween even during winter, but the sky was still clear.

The rumble came again, followed by a shriek. I was instantly on my feet. Kur shot from the trees, his wings flapping furiously. He landed on my shoulder and grappled for a hold on my jacket.

Another beast burst from the trees. It was taller than a man, with shaggy hair the color of a March snowbank covering its entire body. Black eyes peered through a matted fringe over a heavy brow. It raised its arms, pounded fists at the night and yelled, "ROAR!"

Bone-white fangs glistened in the moonlight and spittle sprayed over the snow.

I'd left my sword by my bedroll, and I struggled to pull my knife from my belt. Avie didn't hesitate. She swung the shovel and clobbered the beast over the head, then spun and drove the shovel into its gut.

The beast hissed as it tried to suck in air. Avie struck again. The creature shielded its head with shaggy arms, but Avie wouldn't let up. Her toque flew off in the frenzy as she swung the shovel over and over again. The beast yelped like a scared puppy. Finally, it gave up the fight and stumbled away, tripping right through our camp and over a fire, scattering embers and sending sparks billowing into the sky.

Blaster fire from the soldiers on watch followed its trail as it ran into the dark.

In the silence that followed, the trees creaked as frozen trunks rubbed together.

Avie's fingers were still clamped around the shovel. Her cheeks were damp and flushed and she panted.

"Was that a snowman?" she asked.

"Abominable," I confirmed.

"Did he actually say 'roar'?"

Then the wine and adrenaline got to us and we dissolved into giggles.

Kur must have thought I was having a seizure. He jumped on my chest and grabbed my cheeks in his tiny blue paws to peer right into my eyes.

"Well, that'll teach 'em to interrupt our girls' weekend." Avalon hiccuped.

A Snowman by Any Other Name...

January 1, 2083

Happy New Year! As everyone in my family is still sleeping off the festivities of the last week, I find myself awake and in possession of something really rare: spare time. So, I thought I'd update the blog. It's been a while, I know, and I'm sorry for that. Being a new mom is as life-changing as they say it is. But today I have a few moments to tell you about an amazing creature I encountered recently—a yeti.

That's right, the good old, abominable snowman.

Every mountainous region on Terra seems to have stories about hairy, primeval, humanoid creatures who only get photographed with blurry lenses. Sometimes, these creatures are shy and docile. Sometimes they are aggressive and warrior-like.

Yeti is the term for the Tibetan version of this mountain man-ape. In North America, the most famous man-ape is the Sasquatch. Or at least that was before the Flood Wars. Since then the berserkers, found all over the Adirondack Mountains, have entered the modern lore, mostly as vicious bandits that rove in gangs, attacking homesteaders.

The Barbegazi are said to dwell in the snowy peaks of the Alps, and the Chuchuna ranges through Siberia.

So it's safe to say that most of these creatures have been around for centuries, long before the first cracks in the veil brought the berserkers and other new species. Where did they come from? Are they a genetic mutation of homo sapiens? Perhaps we'll never know.

As I mentioned, I encountered a yeti in the Inbetween just before Christmas. He gave us a good scare, but thinking back on the encounter, perhaps we startled him as much as he startled us. He didn't put up much of a fight. Poor guy. He was probably out for an evening stroll in the snow when he stumbled over our camp.

If you have any yeti/Bigfoot/Barbegazi stories, I'd love to hear them.

COMMENTS (5)

Have you ever heard of the Yowie from Aus? Glowing red eyes, big hairy feet. He's a tough bugger. Tastes good on the barbie though.
BigRoo455 (January 1, 2083)

———•——

May the new year bring you an abundance of blessings!
cchedgewitch (January 1, 2083)

> And to you too, my friend.
> *Valkyrie367 (January 1, 2083)*

———•——

I will love him and hug him and name him George.
OneWorld888 (January 1, 2083)

> OneWorld888, you won the Ley-net today.
> *Valkyrie367 (January 1, 2083)*

CHAPTER

8

ur caravan stopped at a crossroads. Turning left led you down an ominous looking track, no more than a scratch in the ice. That way lay dragons. To the right stretched a well-traveled road of hard-packed snow that led to Annequin Lodge.

I'd visited the lodge on my first journey with Mason into the Inbetween. The innkeeper's daughter had treated me for vampire venom. Despite my horrific ordeal at the hands (and fangs) of the opji, I remembered my time at Annequin with fondness. It was a warm, welcoming place. A perfect place for Avie to wait for us while we went in the other direction to face dragons.

"No way," Avie said, when Carmen suggested it. She slouched in the back seat with her arms crossed. "I came all this way, I want to see dragons."

"It's not safe," Carmen said.

"Liar. You said we would be protected."

"That was before we lost two transports." Carmen glared at her in the rearview mirror.

In the end, those lost transports were the deciding factor. After conferring with McCabe, they decided that it was too risky to split the smaller caravan, so we all headed for the bulla and the dragons.

Avie smirked like she'd won a personal victory.

"You just do as I say when we get there." Carmen's eyes flicked to her in the rearview mirror. "If anything happens to you, Trevor will hunt me down."

The trunk plunged down the snowy track that was no wider than a logging road. I saw recently razed stumps of enormous pines on either side. R&H

Reclamation had cleared it not too long ago, probably when the bulla first appeared. In the spring, brush would reclaim it, and they'd struggle to keep the road open. The van's skis hit boulders and roots hidden under the snow, and we were jostled around like a barrel of monkeys.

Avie leaned forward to hang onto the front seats.

"So what are they like? Dragons, I mean. Do they really breathe fire? How does that work? What does it sound like when they talk inside your head?"

Carmen glanced at me, as if to say, "You're up."

"Yes, they do breathe fire. I'm not sure exactly what the mechanics of it are, but they eat magic, so that might have something to do with it." I tried to answer her questions in order. "As for speaking with them, it's kind of like talking to yourself in your head, only different."

Avie snorted. "Well, that's doesn't tell me much. Do you think they would speak to me? That would be incredible."

"I don't know. Maybe."

"You're not getting close enough to try," Carmen said.

Avie stuck out her tongue. Carmen saw it in the rear-view mirror and said, "Nice. Real mature."

Avie slumped back again. "That's what happens when you spend all your time with humans under the age of sixteen."

Ten minutes later, the caravan slid to a stop. Ahead, a mound of rubble blocked the road.

"We walk from here," Carmen said.

The motion of the van had lulled Kur to sleep. I zipped up my jacket and nudged him. He chirped and jumped up, wide awake and ready to face his next adventure. I wished I had his enthusiasm for the job. Dragons were unpredictable. So were bullas. And the weather? I glanced at the sky. It was as sharp and clear as an ice chip. But that could change in an instant.

The soldiers were already climbing the pile of rubble made up of broken concrete, rocks and clumps of frozen dirt.

"Did the dragons do that?" Avie asked. Her voice seemed too loud in the quiet and she winced.

"Not the dragons," Carmen said. "It's the boundary of the bulla."

I'd seen this kind of upheaval. When Terra spat forth a bulla, it erupted from the depths of the earth, leaving the surrounding terrain untouched. This disturbance of rock and concrete was the demarcation line.

"The road won't be cleared until the dragons let up." Carmen squinted into the bright sky. "We lost an entire team to their attacks already."

Avie followed her gaze. She shivered and not from the cold. Right then, she was imagining those dragons dive-bombing us.

"You could wait in the van," I whispered.

Avie shook her head, but her air of defiance was gone. Good. Cockiness got people killed.

We climbed over the rubble and finally stood on bulla grounds. A ten-acre clearing stretched before us with a massive factory standing in the middle of it. Wind whipped snow off the ground and tossed it in circles.

Terra had coughed up a long, boxy building of poured concrete and metal siding, and it reminded me of how ugly parts of our old world had once been. A series of massive garage doors with loading docks lined the right half of the building. One door was crushed inward, revealing the dark interior. Giant wooden spools lay stacked beside the loading bays, ready to be refilled with finished copper wire.

The other half of the building was faced with opaque office windows. Something was perched on the corner of the roof. I dug my binoculars out of my pack. The figure perched on the roof was an owl. It sat perfectly still. I watched for a full minute and decided it was one of those decoys meant to keep birds from crashing into the windows. What a blast from the past. There wasn't much in the Inbetween that would be scared off by a fake owl.

I scanned the rest of the building but saw no movement through any window. I lowered the binoculars.

"Where are they?" I couldn't say exactly why I whispered. The dragons had to know we were there.

"Inside. Sheltering from the cold, I suppose." Carmen pointed to the ruined garage door. Then she turned to lay a map on the hood of the truck. It wasn't the original builder's schematics. Those were lost to time. This was a draft of the factory done by the scouts who originally claimed the bulla for R&H.

"With the dragons inside, we can't get at the copper." She pointed to the middle section of the building. "Our scouts reported that the coils of fully annealed copper are here. And in the back section there's a huge supply of raw copper rods."

A scout returned to report that the dragons were squatting on the factory floor behind the loading bay.

Carmen pointed to that section on the map.

"So what's the plan?" I asked.

"The plan is you and I go in and try to negotiate with the queen. If things go sour, I have soldiers placed around the perimeter, and they'll shower the place with explosives. We'll extract the copper from the wreckage."

She left important details out of that plan. Like the fact that the explosives would bring the building down on our heads.

"I should go in alone," I said.

"Nope." Carmen didn't even look at me, but I wasn't letting go that easily.

"I can handle myself."

"I don't doubt that. I've heard the stories. This isn't about you. It's an insurance thing. R&H needs to be covered in case...you know."

"In case the dragons burn me to a cinder."

"Exactly."

"Fine. But while we're in there, I'm in charge. I'll defer to you in everything else, but when we face the dragons, I do the talking."

"That's why you're here."

"Great!" Avie piped up. "Can I come."

We both turned to her and shouted, "No!"

WE RETURNED TO the van to gear up. Carmen packed on weapons—knives and a hand-blaster. None of those would kill a dragon, but she probably felt more secure with them strapped to her belt. I took only my sword and my usual kit.

Before we'd left Montreal, I'd asked Carmen to round up some strong magical artifacts for trading with the dragons. I sorted through them in the trunk of the van and chose three that made my keening sizzle. One was a dragonfly pendant, old and humming with spicy magic. The second was a child's toy—a small wooden train. Its magic wept like a lament, but it was potent. The final object was the skull of an infant. It was cracked and browned with age. I didn't need to touch it to sense the miasma of dark magic oozing from its sightless eyes. I hesitated to include it, but magic was magic. Dark or light, it would feed the dragons.

Once we were kitted up, we crossed the open expanse of ground toward the factory. Swirls of snow tugged at our ankles. The wind was breathtakingly cold, and my eyes responded by leaking hot tears down my cheeks. My back itched, knowing that a dozen soldiers had their sights pointed in our direction.

"So how does this mind-speak thing work?" Carmen asked in a low voice. "Will you be able to reach out to the queen?"

"Maybe."

Ruby was the only dragon I'd ever spoken to. She was the young red queen I'd saved from a life of slavery. I didn't know if a strange dragon would speak to me.

"I think they understand our language, but their vocal cords can't reproduce it. The mindspeak is their workaround. But that's just a theory. If the queen wants to speak to us, she will. If not…" I didn't want to voice the alternative.

We walked on, snow crunching under our feet. Kur sat on my shoulder, his earlier excitement gone. He was subdued and cuddled close to my ear.

The magic artifacts in my pack whispered at me, a slithery sound that tugged at my attention. As we neared the open garage, I let out my keening and sensed the presence of dragons, but I couldn't tell how many. Their magic was too big and too wild to pinpoint.

A set of rusted stairs led up to the loading bay. I tested the first step with my foot, and it took my weight without shifting. I climbed. Carmen waited until I reached the top and followed.

Inside, we let our eyes adjust to the sudden gloom and got our bearings. The ceiling was high enough to be lost in shadow, giving the space a cavernous feel. More giant empty spools were piled haphazardly to one side of the bay. A forklift was parked in the open space as if the operator had just stepped away for lunch.

The metal stairs groaned behind me and a soldier jumped into the bay. Three more followed.

"I thought you said you and me only!" I hissed at Carmen.

"Insurance," she mouthed back.

I glanced at the soldiers who were fanning out behind us with blasters primed. They wore black body armor with the R&H logo on a shoulder patch. Clearly, they'd never faced dragons before. The armor wouldn't fend off a dragon claw. All it would do was act as a nice roasting oven when dragon fire hit them.

I was considered making a stand against going in hot like this, when from beyond the shipping bay came a loud, sandpapery sound. A claw against cement floor? Nothing else moved. I couldn't see past the pile of spools. I turned back to the loading door, but the soldiers had already slipped into the shadows to take up offensive positions.

The dragons were all around us. I couldn't see them, but I heard them. The slight wheeze of enormous lungs working in the closed space. The settling of leathery wings against scales. And I keened them—hot, wild magic that was distinctively dragon.

Crates and coils had spilled off metal shelves that rose to the ceiling and blocked the view to the rest of the warehouse. Carmen's expression was shut down tight, but she nodded for us to continue around the shelves. Her right hand rested on the blaster at her hip. My sword was still sheathed on my back. It hummed in reply to the magic brooding in the air and the whispering artifacts in my pack.

We rounded the wall of shelves and found the queen.

She was bigger than all five of our caravan trucks together and covered in blood-red scales. With her back to us, all I could see was her tail gracefully arced around...

...a clutch of eggs.

Oh, dear All-father. I shut my eyes and cursed under my breath.

"What's the matter?" Carmen whispered.

"You didn't tell me they were nesting."

"I didn't know. It makes a difference?"

About as different as asking Dr. Jekyll for tea and getting Mr. Hyde, I thought, but only said, "Stay back and stay quiet."

Kur chirped and jetted off my shoulder.

A trigger-nervous soldier opened fire at the ceiling. Kur squawked and dove into the shadows.

The queen hissed and lowered the bulk of her head over her eggs.

A great brown dragon emerged from the shadows and sprayed the room with fire.

I dove behind the metal shelves. Carmen was right behind me.

More blaster fire echoed through the factory.

Damn and *damn.*

I grabbed Carmen's arm and shook it. "Tell them to stop shooting before the whole place goes up in flames!

Carmen spoke into her fancy earpiece. "Cease fire!"

The blasters faded. A dragon roared from somewhere deep inside the factory.

A pile of wooden spindles burned, and smoke filled the air, but the factory was mostly cement and metal and the dragon fire had done little damage.

I worried about Kur, but could do nothing about him now.

I poked my head from behind the wall of shelves. The queen had turned to face us. Her tail still circled her clutch. The brown dragon and another green flanked her like bodyguards. The blaster fire hadn't fazed them, but they were wary. Only half the size of the queen, they stood on back legs with their wings fanned slightly as if they were ready to pounce.

The silence was oppressive. I had to make a move now, before things really got out of hand.

I stepped into the open. The queen watched me approach with hooded eyes.

I shot a glance at Carmen. "Tell your men to keep their sticky fingers off the triggers or we're all toast."

Carmen nodded and spoke low and fast into her mic.

I faced the queen again and let down my personal wards to give her a taste of my magic. At the same time, I risked sending out my keening. Her nostrils flared ever so slightly. Was that recognition in her eyes? Could it really be? What were the chances of meeting her again after two years? But then, how many dragon thunders could there be nearby?

"Ruby?" My voice fell flat in the large, open space.

The brown dragon rumbled out a growl and leaned in to roast me. The queen hissed and he paused. She locked gazes with him, and after a moment, he slunk back into the shadows.

I took that as a good sign.

"Ruby, is that you?"

The queen shifted, pulling her tail more tightly around the eggs.

My name is Kalindarixatlajitaxama. The voice boomed in my head.

"But you once let me call you Ruby, isn't that right?"

She watched me like I was a bug.

I remember you, Kyra of the Green and your noisy sword.

I could almost feel my blade squirming to be let loose.

"Is she talking to you?" Carmen hissed from right behind me. I shushed her with a slash of my hand. Why, oh why hadn't she stayed hidden?

The tip of Ruby's tail—no Kalindarixatlajitaxama's tail—thumped against the floor.

I stepped forward again and bowed my head to show respect.

"May I call you Queen Kalindari?"

The dragon huffed out a response that I took for a yes, then leaned forward. I felt her hot breath snuffle my scalp. I froze in place, though every cell in my body urged me to run. Her breath crept down my neck, my breast, and lingered on my stomach before the great head retreated.

You are different, Kyra of the Green. Your magic is bigger. You have borne offspring.

"Yes. I have a daughter."

Kalindari snorted. I didn't know if my answer pleased her or not.

I became aware of more dragons lurking in the shadows behind the queen, and then a small golden head poked over the ridge of her tail.

He was tiny, smaller even than Ollie had been when I first met him. His frail wings pumped as he tried to leverage himself over the massive tail. He plopped down among the clutch of eggs. Kalinda snagged his head in her mouth.

My heart seized until I saw that her grip was gentle. She moved him away from the eggs and dropped him in the crease between her front legs. The youngling squirmed and fussed until she nudged him with her nose and he settled. Within moments, he was asleep against the scales of her chest.

My son, a gold!

Her words were infused with pride. I also got a fleeting image of sorrow and pain.

"He's beautiful." I didn't know much about dragon babies, but this one seemed odd. His head was too big for his body. Or his body was too fragile to support his head.

"May I show you a picture of my baby."

I see your offspring. She is never far from your thoughts.

Interesting. So Kalindari could receive as well as project thoughts.

We all stood silently watching the baby sleep with his head tucked under his mother's claw. The only light came from small, filthy windows high on the factory walls. In the gloom, I saw bulky shadows moving into position behind their queen. The aborted battle had made the dragons restless. I had to get this meeting going.

I cleared my throat. "We have come to ask for access to your nesting grounds."

No.

"We won't disturb your nest, but only want the metal stored in this old factory."

No.

She let out a hot puff of air.

I unslung the bag of artifacts and held it out. The power emanating from the bag would be felt even by a mundane. "We brought magic to trade with in good faith." I laid the artifacts on the ground as a gesture of goodwill. Kalindari didn't even glance at them.

No.

Hmmm.

"May I ask why you deny this access?"

Our dragons indulge us while we nest, but they are weary of this confinement. Do not tempt them into anger, Kyra of the Green, for it has been long since they fed.

And you are crunchy and taste good with ketchup, I finished silently.

Kalindari snorted. She'd heard my thought. Of course, I knew dragons didn't eat human flesh, but that didn't mean she wouldn't barbecue me for fun.

We watched each other. We were at an impasse.

Finally, Kalindari dipped her snout so her massive eyes were level with mine.

We do not trade. It is a weakness. Humans are not friends.

These thoughts had a strange echo in my head as if they were broadcast over a wide bandwidth. Was she putting on a show for the other dragons?

Read the room, I thought. Kalindari might be Queen, but how much authority did she really have over the others?

My dragons indulge me while I nest, she'd said.

The brown paced restlessly behind her. Was Kalindari protecting the eggs from him or from us?

I sighed. Dragon politics were beyond me. I changed tactics.

"Once, great Kalindari, you let me ride on your back. You saved me from captivity, just as I saved you."

There. A little flattery and a little reminder of past favors.

She watched me with sharp, golden eyes.

Carmen's head swiveled back and forth between us as she tried to keep up with the one-sided conversation.

Finally, Kalindari snorted out hot air that blew over me like a blast from a furnace. She turned her massive head away as if to dismiss me, but her thoughts were clearly implanted in my mind at the same time.

Kyra of the Green did us a great service by freeing us from slavery. But we returned that favor in your battle with the vampires. Our debt is paid. We owe nothing.

I acknowledged her words with a slight bow.

"The only debt I hope to claim is that of friendship."

Her great golden gaze landed on me again. Fleeting images of our time together flashed through my head—riding through the waterfall portal between worlds, fighting off poachers, circling the pen where they'd been held captive in Underhill while archers blasted arrows at us. I couldn't tell if these were my memories or hers.

The clattering sound of falling crates came from the shadows, and a blue dragon burst into the light. Kur clung to his neck, riding just behind the bony crest on his head. The dragon tripped over Kalindari's tail, coming precariously close to squashing the eggs. She hissed. Smoke blasted him. The blue dragon squawked and back-pedaled. His wings flapped and kicked up dust. He rose a few feet off the ground, then thumped down right in front of me. He stretched his wings and let out a mighty caw before tucking his huge nose into the crook between my chin and neck.

Kur squealed and flapped his wings.

Hesitantly, I reached for the bony scales on the dragon's forehead.

"Ollie?"

CHAPTER

9

ur was chirping and flapping and squawking. Ollie hopped up and down and bumped my shoulder with his head. Behind me, Carmen yelled something incoherent. Kalindari had risen from her nest to loom over us all. Behind her, the brown hissed and filled the air with smoke.

I was crying tears of joy.

"Ollie?"

The big blue nose snuffled, and I felt hot breath on my chin. His magic, so familiar to me, soared with happiness. I couldn't resist the urge to hug him. Kur was just as excited to greet his old friend. The three of us must have looked ridiculous, bobbing and chirping, flapping and hugging.

"What's going on?" The anxiety in Carmen's tone finally got through to me.

I stepped back and wiped my eyes. "It's okay. This is Ollie. He's—was one of my rescues."

Carmen eyed the dragon. Ollie now stood over eight feet tall. From nose to tail, he was longer than our truck.

"How'd you fit him into your house?"

I laughed. "He was a lot smaller back then." Part of me missed the adorable baby dragon with his crest of fluffy feathers and stumpy wings, but seeing how he'd grown into this magnificent creature warmed my heart. This was the reason I rescued. If I could rehabilitate one creature and know he'd thrive in the wild, I'd done my job.

Kalindari made a dragon noise deep in her throat. Ollie straightened like he'd been jerked on a string. He lowered his head. She glared at him. They seemed to be communicating on some level I couldn't understand. Finally, Ollie bowed low. Kalindari turned her back to us and circled her eggs protectively, dragging her little gold baby into her embrace too.

Come. Come with me!

Ollie's voice popped into my head. It was like hearing Kalindari, but distinctly different. Oral voices have different pitches and tones. So does mindspeak. But I'd never heard Ollie in my head. He spoke faster than the queen, and my brain translated his tone in a higher pitch.

He trotted—as much as a creature the size of a minivan can trot—toward the light of the loading bay. Kur clung to his shoulders, his tiny claws scrambling for purchase on the blue scales. Ollie didn't seem to mind. Carmen and I followed them.

Outside, sun glinted off the blaster rifles pointing our way.

"Tell your people to stand down," I said to Carmen. She paused. "Do it now!" She nodded and hurried away, talking into her com.

I turned back to Ollie. Kur stood on the bony crest of his head. Wind whipped the ice-sprite's feathery fur into a poof ball. Both stared at me with open, eager expressions, like I might have treats in my pocket. I didn't. Instead, I indicated to Ollie that we should move around the building out of the wind and out of R&H's line of sight. We found a little alcove where employees probably once spent their lunch breaks or slipped out for a quick cigarette.

"I'm really glad to see you." I dared to reach out and scratch the ridge behind his ear. As a baby, he'd loved that. He still did. His eyes half-closed and he leaned into my fingers. Kur cooed and batted at my hand.

"You look really good. Strong and fit."

Ollie cocked his head. I took a deep breath and went for broke.

"I need your help. Those people back there want to trade with your queen, but she won't let them."

Ollie fidgeted.

I speak not against Kalindarixatlajitaxama.

"No! I wouldn't have you speak against her. She is your queen. She's good to you?"

He bowed his head which I took for a yes. Kalindari had once left him behind because his stunted wings couldn't keep up with the other dragons when they escaped. She would do it again if she had to. Dragons were loyal, but they were also brutally pragmatic. I suspected Kalindari was a tough but fair leader.

"I don't want you to go behind her back."

Ollie looked behind him, not understanding.

"I mean I don't want you to go against her wishes or keep secrets."

Another bow.

"Good. I just want you to help me understand why she won't trade with us. We only want the copper coils. They are worthless to the thunder."

Ollie considered the question for a long while. Kur was busy picking dirt or bugs from the crevices between Ollie's scales and eating them.

Finally Ollie seemed to come to some decision.

You will help her? Help Kalindarixatlajitaxama?

"Help her?"

His eyes were big pools of concern. He loved her. And he was afraid for her.

"Of course I'll help. Any way I can."

Images inundated my mind. First, the little gold dragon, just born and as fragile as a baby bird. Then more hatchlings, some alive for only minutes, others too weak to make it out of their shells. Then the scenery changed, and I saw another clutch of eggs. This one on a mountain cliff. Many dragons gathered around them. I could feel their rage and sadness. The eggs were dead.

Another clutch—a few stragglers that died after their first breath and more dud eggs.

Ollie's little montage of dragon baby horrors went on. When it finally stopped, I sagged back against the factory's wall.

By the gods, how long had poor Kalindari been trying? How many times had she watched her babies die? No wonder she was so fiercely proud and protective of the frail little gold.

Then another thought came to me. Ollie had been a fragile fledgeling too, but he'd been stunted by the null collars the poachers had forced them to wear. Wasn't it safe to assume that Kalindari had also been affected by the collars? She'd been a young female then. What if the null magic had damaged her reproductive system?

"She's protective of her babies, isn't she?"

Yesssss. The word came like a hiss in my thoughts. Kalindari wasn't against trading with R&H. She didn't want anyone near her fragile eggs.

More images flew through my head. Dragons sleeping and moping around the factory. Dragons fighting each other. Dragons snapping even at their queen. Kalindari wanted her thunder close to protect her eggs, but the dragons were one fiery breath away from rebellion.

Bored. Soooo bored! Want to fly. Fly free!

Ollie was getting agitated again. I patted his shoulder.

"I understand. I will help. I promise. I have to go, but I'll be back in two days. Keep the others from violence until then. Can you do that?"

I hugged him. I didn't want to go, but I had to if I wanted to save his thunder.

I grabbed Kur and rushed back to the waiting trucks.

"What happened?" Carmen asked.

"We have to get back to Annequin Lodge. And fast." I was already jumping into the truck.

"Are they going to trade?"

"That's depends on how fast your couriers can get us the things I need from Montreal."

CHAPTER

10

nnequin Lodge was exactly as I remembered it. We arrived near dusk, and the fieldstone inn seemed to blend seamlessly with the fading countryside. Maybe that's why Terra let it stand for so long. It seemed less manmade and more organically grown.

The main house and out buildings were surrounded by a stone wall, but the real protection came from an old ward that had been dug deep into the ground by years of magical reinforcement. Only one gate led through this ward—one gate to defend in case of an attack.

I'd given Carmen my list of requests for the dragons during our drive to the inn. As soon as we arrived, she headed to her room to connect her Ley-line link to the R&H headquarters in Montreal. Avie had fallen asleep in the van. I dragged her groggy ass inside and plunked it down at a table beside the hearth in the great room. Kur curled up beside her.

Hearne strolled up to our table. The innkeeper hadn't changed either. His fae blood kept him looking fifty years old, slightly balding, and paunchy. He didn't bother with a glamor, and the nubs of two small horns protruded from his curly hair.

"What'll it be, ladies?"

We ordered warm apple cider and a plowman's plate to share. We'd have dinner with Carmen later, but the day had already been long and I was starving.

While we waited for our food, Avie turned in her chair to stretch her feet toward the fire.

"Oh, that feels good."

"After we eat, I'm going to call home. You should too. Let Trevor know where you are."

Avie shrugged, her eyes fixed on the fire. "Maybe."

"It's okay to be the first one to reach out, you know. There's no shame in missing home."

I didn't want Avie's stubbornness to sabotage her relationship. But she only mumbled something incoherent, and I left her to mull it over in peace. I had my own family to miss.

I sipped my cider, letting the heat from the fire soothe me, until I keened a sudden surge of magic beside me.

Avie went rigid like she'd been shot with five-hundred volts of electricity. Her knuckles turned white, clenching the chair arms. Her eyes rolled back in her head, and a voice boomed from her throat with otherworldly authority.

"When steel turns to rust and bodies rain from the sky, a child in red will bring the black death of truth!"

Then she slumped into her chair like a deflated balloon.

"Wha—? Did you sh..say something?" She slurred and wiped a bit of drool off her chin with a shirt sleeve.

"You did." I pulled out my widget and jotted down her words before I forgot them.

"Prophecy?" she asked.

"Uh-huh."

Every so often, some higher power used Avie like a megaphone. I'd been keeping track, trying to find some common thread, but so far, the prophecies seemed random.

"What did I say?"

I told her.

"Damn. That's the third one this week." Avie rubbed the side of her head.

"Really? What were the other ones about?"

"Dunno. I was alone with the kids. Something about the air turning white and gray. You think it has something to do with the dragons?"

"Doubt it. Probably just some etheric mumbo-jumbo. Like radio static on a higher frequency." That was my current theory, anyway.

"Yeah, probably." Avie forced a smile.

In my experience, prophecies were generally about as useful as a screaming into a storm. But the fact that Avie's prognostications were coming so frequently made me pause. Her murky messages from the beyond didn't feel like static. They felt heavy. Ominous. Like something was watching and waiting for the right time to strike.

Hearne saved us from falling into the trap of trying to dissect the nonsensical prophecy when he returned with two steaming mugs of cider.

"What's the news from around here?" I asked.

"Been quiet."

"No opji activity?" I tried to make the question sound casual, but I still had nightmares about being bitten. I might have died if Hearne's daughter hadn't been so adept at old-fashioned healing.

"Nah. The vamps have been quiet this season." He paused and looked out the only window by the front door. "Though I don't know how long that'll last. I heard rumors of a big upset in Vioska. A coup. Lots of infighting and a new leader."

"How would you hear that?" It wasn't like the opji allowed visitors to their ward. The only humans who went there never came out.

"Traders." Hearne grunted. "The opji aren't entirely self-sufficient. They still need to barter for certain goods."

"Wow. I wouldn't want to be one of those traders."

"Nor me. It would take some big brass balls to willingly walk into a vamp den." He smiled and I instantly felt lighter and more rested. I wondered if that was a bit of innkeeper magic at work.

After we ate, I told Avie I wanted to check on Carmen and see if she was able to secure the items I'd requested. I also needed to call Mason.

Avie mumbled incoherently and went back to zoning out on the warmth and light play from the fire. She had things to work out and there was no better place to do that than in front of Annequin's hearth.

I slipped away and found Carmen in her room. She was in the middle of a call, but she waved me in. The screen on her small computer showed a black-haired women with deep lines between her brows, as if she'd frowned too much in her life and the expression had stuck.

"How long will those damned dragons be nesting?" The woman asked.

"Hard to say. Could be months." Carmen kept her tone deferential.

"We don't have months! *You* don't have months! I'm giving you a week. If

I don't have my copper by then, you don't have a job." The screen went blank as the woman cut the connection.

"I'm glad we didn't invite her on our girls' weekend," I said.

"Amen to that." Carmen rubbed the bridge above her brows. "At least she agreed to send what we need. Are you sure it will be enough?"

"It's worth a try."

Carmen nodded. Her thoughts were clearly a mile away.

"Hey," I said. "I was hoping to get a line out to Mason, to warn him that R&H couriers will be coming to collect a few things."

"Of course. You probably want to check in on that baby too."

"Yes." Just thinking about Holly made my boobs ache. I'd have to express milk before dinner or I'd leak all over the table.

Carmen punched in a code and a new screen popped up.

"Just put in the address," she said. "I'll leave you alone."

A minute later, Mason's face appeared on the screen. He was unshaven, tousle-haired and absolutely gorgeous. Holly's little face was visible at the bottom of the screen. She was sound asleep and tucked into the crook of Daddy's shoulder. I knew that spot. There was no more comfortable place on Terra. A sudden, sharp longing for home hit me.

Mason's eyes sparkled when he said, "Hey, you."

"Hey, you." My throat closed on tears. I wouldn't let them out. By the All-father, I'd only been gone a day! I could do this. My life didn't have to always revolve around Mason and Holly.

But damn, they were beautiful.

"How's it going?" he asked.

"Okay. You won't believe who I met today." I told him about Ruby (now Kalindari) and the conundrum of getting the copper out from under the nesting dragons. And then I told him about Ollie, so grown up and striking.

"Ollie?" Mason's face softened in a grin. "I'm glad he made it out there."

I nodded. "He looks good. Strong and sleek." Mason understood the bitter-sweetness I felt when I had to give up one of my rescues for a better life out in the wild.

Next I told him about my plan and what R&H couriers would be coming to pick up.

"Are you sure?" His lips pursed in a slight frown, and I wished I could shove my head through the screen to kiss him.

"I'm sure. Can you have them ready?"

"Of course."

"I'll be gone a few extra days." I held my breath before I said more. I wouldn't apologize or complain.

"I know." His words were soft. "We'll be fine." He kissed the top of her fuzzy head.

"I wanted to be back in time for Christmas, but…" I looked away.

"Kyra, don't worry. It's just a date on the calendar. Christmas and all its trappings will be waiting for you when you get home. So will we."

There was a pause full of unsaid words. We didn't need to say them. I knew he loved me and missed me. And he knew how I felt. It was enough to feel that connection even through a video.

"So how're things there?" I asked.

"Same old, same old. The godlings sparked a riot at a supposedly peaceful rally last night."

"Was anyone hurt?"

"Yes, but no one killed."

Thank the gods whose offspring were all idiots.

"And Raven? Is he okay?"

Mason smiled. "Don't worry. I've kept him too busy to get into trouble." He leaned forward and whispered, "we're working on a super-secret project. A Christmas gift for you."

"I can't wait to see it." I smiled through blurry eyes.

Holly woke with a tiny snort. She snuffled around for a moment, then started to cry. The reaction was instantaneous. My milk came down in a hot, aching rush and soaked my shirt.

Holly howled.

"I'd better go feed the little beast," Mason said over the noise.

I nodded and blew him a kiss. He disconnected. I sat staring at the black screen, getting a hold of my emotions. After a moment, I sniffled and went to my room to change into a dry shirt.

CHAPTER

11

O n Christmas Day, we stood on the edge of the bulla again. We'd returned as soon as our requested supplies arrived from Montreal. In the time we'd been gone, R&H workers had cleared the road and set up a trailer in the factory's parking lot to act as a command center. Another convoy of soldiers had arrived. This one included armored transports and a missile launcher. They weren't fooling around anymore. Getting the dragons to deliver the goods peacefully was my responsibility, and never before had my job weighed so heavily on me.

The sun shone high and white in a pale blue sky. The tip of my nose was already frozen, and I stamped my feet to keep them warm as I scanned the factory.

The dragons were quiet and the building was dark. But right now, I was more concerned with the parking lot. It was level and wide enough for what I wanted, but snow covered it in drifts that rose to the height of a man in some places. For my plan to work, we needed ice, not snow.

As soon as we'd arrived, I'd sent Kur into the factory to find Ollie. Now, Ollie came half flying, half running outside with Kur riding shotgun on his head. Ollie skidded to a stop in front of the command center. I heard a few muffled curses from the soldiers, but Carmen had warned them to leave their weapons cold.

After explaining to Kur and Ollie what I wanted, I leaned against an R&H truck to watch.

Carmen walked over from the trailer and handed me a mug of coffee.

Gods, I was going to miss coffee when this job was done. I wrapped my hands around the hot java goodness and watched Ollie and Kur confer over the snow drifts in a series of chirps and trills that sounded like baby-talk.

"Do you really think this will work?" Carmen asked.

"Just watch." I nodded toward the open lot. They'd finally sorted themselves out. Kur perched on the tip of Ollie's tale. The dragon sucked in a breath and let out a billow of flames. He pressed forward, clearing a path through the drifts. As snow melted under his feet, Kur put his particular magic to good use. He screwed up his face, spread his little fingers and pointed at the snowmelt. It froze in a perfect sheet of ice.

Dragon plus ice-sprite makes the perfect Zamboni machine.

I left them to their work and headed inside the factory. It was Christmas Day. I was far from home and my family, but I had a job to do. I had one last shot at convincing the queen to surrender the copper before R&H guns started blazing.

I couldn't keep Carmen or Avie outside.

Avie crossed her arms and planted her feet in front of me. "I came all this way. I'm not going home without seeing a dragon."

"What about Ollie?" I pointed to where the blue dragon was now sliding less than gracefully across the frozen rink.

Avie rolled her eyes. "A real dragon. Not that Labrador with scales."

I looked at Carmen for confirmation. She nodded. "I'll keep her out of the way."

"Fine. But the only soldiers inside are the ones bringing the goods. Agreed?"

"Agreed." Carmen glanced at her widget. "Let's move. I want to report to head office by noon, and it better be with good news."

She ordered two soldiers to grab the duffle bags of supplies from Montreal and follow us. I shouldered my own backpack with its precious cargo, and we all headed into the loading bay.

I found Kalindari lounging sleepily on her nest. If she knew about the commotion outside, she gave little indication. Her tail still wrapped the clutch of eggs, and her baby slept between her two great paws. I thought his color was appropriate because she hoarded that baby like gold.

Ollie—with Kur still perched on his head—stayed close to Kalindari's side, though he carefully kept away from the eggs. The rest of the thunder—I'd counted four more dragons—moved restlessly in the shadows. The sound of dragon scales sliding against the cement floor as they paced was a constant reminder of their short fuses and my even shorter deadline.

Perfect. I had bored, temperamental dragons in front of me and cold, trigger happy humans at my back.

I stood in the middle of the factory floor feeling very alone.

Kalindari saw me approach. Her sleepy eyes fell on me, and she turned away, pulling her infant with her.

"Great Queen, I come…"

Her head swung around and she struck out like a viper. Flames blasted over my head, and I was suddenly looking up the smoking nose of a pissed off dragon.

Ollie squeaked and hid behind the bulk of Kalindari's tail.

WE DO NOT TRADE WITH HUMANS!

I slammed my hands over my ears, even though that did nothing to quiet the echo of the queen's shout inside my mind.

She puffed out another hot breath that singed the pompom on my toque.

I held my hands in front of me as if trying to gentle a wild fawn and not a raging dragon.

"Please, I don't come to trade. Only to share a story." My words were true, but while I spoke, I focused my thoughts. I didn't want Carmen and the others to hear what I had to say. Instead, I tested my mindspeak abilities and filled my thoughts with images of soldiers, tanks and the missile launcher all waiting outside. I needed Kalindari to understand that the humans were ready to storm her nest.

Please let me help you. I can make the humans go away and leave you in peace to hatch your young. All I ask is for you to listen to my story.

I repeated the words in my head several times, not sure of how well my mindspeak translated to the dragon. Kalindari watched me through hooded eyes, until finally, she gave one last snort and settled back around her eggs.

Speak, Kyra of the Green. Then you will leave or I will burn your bones to ash.

No pressure then.

I glanced over my shoulder once. Carmen had kept her word. Avie stood with her in the shadows. The only others inside were the soldiers carrying the duffle bags. The rest of R&H's little army waited quietly outside. They wouldn't stay quiet for long.

I took a deep breath and faced the queen.

"It's the custom among our people to exchange gifts at this time of year. This tradition has a long history, from ancient Roman emperors who demanded tithes, to benevolent saints who brought alms and food to the poor, to scrooges and grinches who learned to give only after they had taken everything from the people they should love."

I turned so the others could see me. Avie's eyes were wide. Carmen frowned. She wanted to know where I was going with this seemingly random lecture.

"Miracles happen at this time," I continued, "when snow is deepest and spring just a faint memory."

TELL ME OF A MIRACLE!

I winced. By the All-father, I wished she'd stop shouting in my brain.

I frantically sorted through the stories I knew about the Yule season. I hadn't been prepared for specifics. I just wanted her to accept our gifts. But if Queen Kalindari wanted a story, I thought it best to give her one.

I wracked my brain for an appropriate tale. In an age when magic was commonplace, it wasn't easy to impress with so-called miracles. There was the Hanukkah tradition where oil for one night lit the lamps for eight nights, but I didn't think that was enough to rouse the dragons. The baby Jesus and the Magi? They brought gifts. But it wasn't an exchange. The idea of exchange was vital here.

Then a spark of a story came to me. It was something I'd read in ninth-grade history, so it had to be at least partly true. Not that truth mattered in this instance. Or at least it mattered less than inspiration. But telling a lie to a dragon that could look inside your head was never a good idea. I took a gamble. The spirit of the story was true. That had to be enough.

I pushed a bit of magic in my voice so it reached deep into the shadows.

"Once two great armies fought for the right to stand on a sacred hill."

Kalindari's eyes widened and she sat up straighter. Dragons understood battles for territory. Behind her, the others in her thunder were silent. This was the most entertainment they'd had during the long weeks of nesting.

"For days, the armies launched deadly missiles at each other while sheltering in fortifications dug from the ground." A dragon snorted. No dragon would ever hide in a trench. "Thousands of men died in the cold and the wet, far away from their families and homes. The land between them was slick with mud and red from blood. No one dared to step on it, not even to recover their dead."

Kalindari made a guttural noise. I wasn't sure if she was bored or intrigued. I forged ahead anyway.

"December 25th dawned wet and foggy, and the spirit of Christmas settled over the battlefield. No bombs were launched that day. Instead, the men rose from the trenches, and the two armies met on the bloody field to exchange gifts. They had little to give—an extra packet of tea, unbroken boot laces, cigarettes. The armies spoke different languages. It didn't matter. They understood the language of kindness and friendship—of giving and receiving. As the sun rose, someone made a ball from rags, and the two armies played football in the mud. On that day, no one won or lost, and no one died. When the sun went down, they shook hands and returned to their fortifications on either side of the hill."

I thought I had the gist of the story right even if I'd embellished the details. An image of dragons facing off in a muddy field popped into my mind. Fire replaced bombs and roars replaced gunfire. Of course, Kalindari would translate my words into her terms. That was fine. The story transcended race or even species. At least I had caught the queen's imagination.

Did the armies continue to fight and kill each other after that day?

Kalindari shoved her head forward so her snout and one great eye filled my entire field of vision. This question was important to her, and I wasn't sure which answer she wanted to hear. Would she rather believe the spirit of Christmas was powerful enough to end a years-long war? Or should I tell her the truth?

I went with the truth.

"Yes, they did."

Good.

I felt her satisfaction in the fact that the war had continued after Christmas was over. Dragon logic. Go figure.

"But in that tradition of peace and friendship on this day, I ask to invoke the true spirit of Christmas. It is the celebration of family and *friends*." I put as much emphasis on that last word as I could. "And it shows how even enemies can become friends, if for a short while."

Kalindari bared a fang in what might have been a smile. Or she might have been getting ready to eat me. I held my ground.

"Today is Christmas Day as marked by the human calendar. And so we return to you, not with a proposal for trade, but with gifts freely given." I waved to the R&H soldiers who dragged the duffle bags forward and dumped them in front of the queen. I unzipped the first one to reveal a dozen pairs of skates, the old fashioned kind that could be strapped over any boot or even—I hoped—over dragon paws. The second bag held hockey sticks and pucks.

"I bring these as gifts for your thunder. They are the tools for a game that is holy to my people. A game of conquering and targeting, and mastery over the elements. We call it ice hockey. It's fast and dangerous, and I believe it will cure your dragons of their ennui. There are more soldiers waiting outside to show your thunder how to play."

I waved a hand at the duffle bags. The soldiers picked them up and headed outside to the make-shift skating rink.

None of the dragons moved. Kalindari watched us with her inscrutable golden eyes. Her mindspeak was silent, and I had no idea what she was thinking. Then she rumbled something at Ollie. He, in turn, snarled at the dragons in the shadows. Three bulky figures slouched toward the loading bay. The last dragon, the brown who was almost as big as Ollie, hissed out smoke and refused to move. Ollie growled and snapped at the brown's heels until they followed the others outside.

Wow. Ollie hadn't just grown up. He was an alpha.

I would have given my left kidney to watch the dragons learn to skate, but I had to finish this now.

"And I have something for you, Queen Kalindari. For you and your son."

Her nose dropped to the little gold dragon sleeping between her paws. Even at rest, he looked frail, like every tiny snore might be his last.

In my bag, I carried the precious gift that I'd sent for. Mason had packed it carefully. Two apples were nestled in a cushion of wool. I held them up in the dim light.

They were apple perfection. Two round orbs with a dimple where the stem sprouted. Red like a summer sunset with a blush of peach.

Kalindari's eyes widened. She sensed the enormity of their magic.

The Aesir fiercely protected the secret of the Golden Apples, so I spoke no words aloud to explain the gift, but I filled my mind with images of my healing in Iduna's orchard, of how I had despaired for the life of my unborn child, until the apples had fortified my body, and kept my womb safe. I impressed her with other miracles of the apples, and how the Aesir had been blessed with their healing magic for a millennium. I projected all these thoughts, hoping Kalindari understood.

I know what it is to fear for your child. Take this gift in good faith—one mother to another. Feed half an apple to your son. It will make him strong. Eat the other half yourself and keep the second apple for your new hatchlings. Feed them each a piece as soon as they hatch. And may the gods bless you with a strong and mighty brood.

I imagined a whole thunder of baby dragons taking flight, soaring in a rainbow hue of shining colors against the setting sun.

I packed the apples away and risked a step forward into the queen's space to put the bag at her feet.

Kalindari scrutinized my every movement. I could feel her eyes boring into me, as if her gaze could turn me inside out, hang me upside down by the ankles and shake secrets from my pockets. But even as her thoughts ferreted through mine, she could find no duplicity in me, only a real desire to help.

A massive red claw shot out and snagged the bag of apples.

Humans! The Queen's voice boomed in my head, imperial and demanding. Carmen and Avie jerked upright as they experienced mindspeak firsthand. *Take your copper. Tomorrow we return to the trenches.*

WE WATCHED SOLDIERS wearing powerful exoskeletons carry the huge coils of copper to waiting trucks.

"How did you get her to agree?" Carmen asked.

I shrugged. "She likes apples."

Carmen squinted at me. She wasn't buying it. "Those must have been some special apples."

"Honey crisps," I said. "Super sweet."

"Uh-huh."

A wave of human shouts came from the far side of the parking lot, followed by a dragon's roar.

"Come on." I tugged on the sleeve of her jacket. "I want to see the end of the game." Carmen waved me off and went to check on the progress of loading the copper. I headed over to our makeshift hockey rink.

Ollie had managed to coax or bully the other dragons onto the ice. I couldn't see the skate blades under their massive feet, but I could hear them carving up the ice as the dragons whirled and glided across the rink.

Five soldiers had been delegated to play hockey with them while the others loaded copper. Carmen had chafed at the delay, but I'd explained that was the price for the dragons' cooperation.

Since everyone else was busy, Avie was the only cheerleader at the game. She stood beside the rink, striking the sky with her fist every time someone shot for the goal.

"Who's winning?" I asked.

"Who cares?" Her face was flushed from the cold and the excitement. "This is the best thing I've ever seen!"

It was pretty cool.

Five men and women had strapped on skates and helmets to face off against five dragons. It was a story they'd tell their grandkids.

There were no goalies, but the nets were small and easily defended. For beings made of fire, the dragons took to the ice like pros. Their bulky bodies were balanced by long tails that they used in place of hockey sticks. They seemed to be enjoying the exercise. If nothing else, the game gave Kalindari time to herself without the thunder of bored dragons breathing down her neck.

A human woman slapped the puck at the dragons' net with a grunt and a fierce grin. Ollie blocked it with his tail and winged in back down the ice. On his shoulder, Kur squealed with glee. It did my heart good to see the little ice-sprite come to life again.

Two dragons clashed over the puck and went sailing into a snowbank. They came up thrashing and puffing smoke.

I could watch them all day, but my home and my family called to me. It was time to go.

Avie grabbed my elbow.

"I want to thank you." Her cheeks were pink from the cold and her eyes bright.

"For what?"

"For this." She waved a mittened hand at the hockey game. "For letting me know dragons are real. Sometimes a girl just needs to believe in something extraordinary."

"Does that mean you're ready to go home."

"Oh, yes. My butt is frozen!" She jumped up and down and hugged herself. "But seriously. I needed time and perspective. This trip gave me both. So thanks."

"Any time. You saved my butt last year. Now I've saved yours."

"Are we keeping score? Cuz if so, I think we both owe Carmen a debt for the coffee." She grinned and headed back toward the trailer and the hot coffee.

I waved to Ollie. He came careening across the ice and skidded to a stop with a shower of ice shavings. I reached up to pat his nose that was puffing out steam.

"I'm so glad I got to see you," I said. "You've grown into a mighty dragon, just like I knew you would."

He ducked his head so I could scratch behind his ear.

"You take care of your queen and the babies." My throat was closing up at the thought of saying goodbye.

"I have to go home now." Ollie whined. Kur chirped. He was still sitting on Ollie's shoulder and flicked his gaze between us. "Kur, you can stay with Ollie if you want. Or you can come home with me."

I held my breath. My rescues weren't my prisoners. I would never make one stay with me if they didn't want to. Kur had been my companion for nearly a decade, but he'd come alive on this trip and I wouldn't deny him his happiness if he wanted to stay with the dragons.

Kur chirped and hopped onto Ollie's head. He took both bony eye-ridges in his tiny hands and pressed his face to Ollie's forehead. Awww. It was an ice-sprite kiss. Then he hopped over to land on my shoulder. He was coming with me. I won't lie. I was relieved.

I patted his fluffy shoulder. "Don't worry. Ollie will come visit us. Won't you Ollie?" The dragon tilted his head. "You remember where Mason's house is, don't you?" I projected the memory of him as a young dragon stopping for a visit on Mason's balcony.

I will come. When my fledglings take flight. His unique voice lilted inside my mind.

His fledglings? I didn't know exactly how dragons reproduced, but I knew only the queen laid eggs. And it seemed that Ollie was their father. How wonderful. A perfect end to a most extraordinary Christmas Day.

I patted him one more time and turned to leave with tears threatening my eyes.

A clawed hand grasped my shoulder and I stopped. Ollie held a brilliant blue dragon scale in one paw, a scale that would have fetched a small fortune on the Black Hat market.

For your baby. May she one day meet mine in friendship.

EPILOGUE

t was good to be home. Mason and the goblits had been busy in my absence. The house was lit with enough colorful gleams that I spied it through the trees as my van wound through the last turns of Dorion Park.

Snow fell in fat, fluffy flakes. Kur slept on the seat beside me, worn out from his adventure. I parked in my usual spot and gently shook him awake.

"We're home, buddy." The ice-sprite yawned and stretched arms and wings. We stepped into the wintery night.

The barn was dark and quiet. All my critters were asleep. I'd check on them later that night, but right now, I couldn't wait any longer to see Holly and Mason.

Three snowmen and a snow dog were lined up in the garden. One of the snowmen had wings. They all wore hats and scarves and greeted me with icy grins.

Soft music was playing inside—old fashioned Christmas carols—and real candles shimmered in the frosted windows.

The front door opened and Mason stepped onto the porch with a bundled baby in his arms. Kur hopped off my shoulder and dashed inside. Holly saw me and stretched, waving mittened hands and gurgling out a frustrated wail.

I grabbed her in a hug. She squirmed, but the wail turned into a satisfied coo. Mommy was home. Everything was right with the world again.

Mason slung an arm around us both and kissed the top of my head. "The Guardians warned us you were coming, but little missy here didn't want to put on her snowsuit."

"Did you fuss?" I flapped one of her mittens and she laughed. "Well, I've had enough of the cold for a while. Let's go inside."

I could see faces pressed against the front windows. Everyone was waiting for me.

Inside, an enormous Christmas tree rose right to the vaulted ceiling. Garlands of fresh pine decorated the rafters, filling the room with their spicy scent. Stockings bursting with candy hung by the hearth where a fire danced. Grim basked in the heat of the flames with Willow tucked at his side.

Tums and Tad, Raven and Princess, Jacoby, Gita with Hunter on her shoulder, and all the other goblins stood by the tree. They were dressed in their Christmas finery. The goblits had combed their hair. Jacoby wore his best vest and new pants. I even spied Cricket, the shy hidebehind, lurking in the shadows behind the tree. They had delayed their Christmas and had all come together for me.

I didn't know what to say. Any words would fall short, and they'd surely be accompanied by a rush of tears. Tums and Tad save me by rushing up and pulling on my hands.

"Look! Look! Miss Kyra." Tums spoke, but Tad hopped up and down. "We made strings of popcorn and painted wooden trains! On the tree. Look!"

I laughed, handed Holly back to Mason, and let them pull me over to the tree. Colorful gleams nestled in its boughs and homemade ornaments hung from every branch.

"You did all this?" I asked.

The twins nodded. "Jacoby and Raven helped too! Raven flew up to the highest branch to put up the star. Look!" He pointed to the gold star gracing the top of the tree.

"It's beautiful." I looked over Tums' head at Raven so he would know I appreciated his effort too. I was just glad that something had finally brought him and the goblits together.

"Food or presents first?" Mason asked.

"Presents!" Raven, Tums and Jacoby all shouted at the same time.

I turned to Mason and he shrugged. "Presents it is, then."

The next hour went by in a blur of laughter and shreds of gift wrapping.

I'd sorted out my presents before I left on my trip and Mason had taken care of the wrapping. There was something for everyone. Jacoby got a new emergency kit with a knife and first aid supplies, and his own widget. Everything an apprentice needed. I'd found a rare hardcover boxed set of the Chronicles of Narnia for Gita. Raven and the goblits got reconditioned mountain bikes for the spring and games and puzzles to keep them busy until then. In the same place I'd found Gita's books, I also found an ancient collection of short stories about First Nations folklore for Raven. His eyes widened when he saw the image of Thunderbird on the cover. He was shy about giving thanks, but he nodded and held the book firmly in both hands like a talisman. I never wanted him to forget his heritage, and this was a small token in that direction.

Holly was spoiled by everyone with toys, homespun blankets and knitted dolls. She was more intrigued with the gift wrappings.

For the older goblins, I'd gone with new boots and coats as well as a few things to make their cottage more comfortable. Grim and Willow were already drooling over catnip stuffed socks, and Princess was making growly noises over a giant bone wrapped in dried bacon. Cricket seemed enthralled with his necklace of gold and silver stars. I'd looped it around his neck and kissed him on the cheek before his shyness got the better of him and he fled to hide behind the tree again.

Mason and I had special gifts for each other. We'd decided to wait and exchange those later in private, but I accepted dozens of other tiny gifts. Each had been made by someone dear. A pair of fingerless gloves for work knitted by Suzt. A new leather knife sheath from Jacoby and a full report—with videos—of the vampire slug birthing from Gibus.

But the best present came from Raven. He waited until almost all the others were open, then shyly handed me a small, flat box tied with green ribbon.

"I made this for you." His hands were shoved deep in his pockets and he wouldn't look at me.

"You did?" I touched the silky ribbon. The super-secret present. What could it be?

I glanced at Mason. He nodded solemnly, but there was a twinkle in his eye. I pulled on the ribbon and the bow came apart. Inside the box, a simple hand-held mirror lay on a bed of tissue paper.

I held up the mirror, curious. Magic crackled though the handle into my palm. This wasn't just a mirror. Then I recognized the runes etched around the frame.

"It's a scrying glass." I was still confused. In Asgard, they used these glasses to communicate images and sound over long distances. On Terra, we had widgets that were much more sophisticated and reliable. Why would I need a scrying glass?

But Raven's grin told me this was something more. He touched a combination of runes and a misty image appeared in the glass.

"I took Mason's tracking beacon—you know the one I brought to Asgard?"

I nodded. That beacon was the only reason Mason had been able to find me.

"Well, I had the idea of combining it with the scrying glass." Now Raven looked sheepish. "I sort of snuck one into my bag before we left Asgard."

I must have looked shocked because he rushed on. "But it's okay. I told Frode. Look."

"You told Frode?" I must have been tired because all this wasn't making sense. Then the swirling mist in the mirror coalesced into the face of King Frode of Asgard.

"Hey, cousin." He grinned, looking more like a mischievous boy than a king. "You've got a hell of a smart kid there. Now we can chat whenever we want. Hey, hey! Don't cry!"

"I'm not." I lied and wiped my damp eyes. "I'm just so happy right now."

I chatted with Frode for a few minutes and we made a scrying date for later in the week, after all the festivities had died down. When my glass turned opaque again, I gently put it back in the box and pulled Raven in for a hug. He only squirmed a bit.

"Thank you. That is the best present I've ever received. You are amazing."

Raven shrugged off the praise. "Mason helped."

"It was all Raven's idea," Mason said. "He's going to change the world one day." He squeezed Raven's shoulder, and I could feel the glow of pride and happiness surrounding them like a cloud.

I sat between my husband and my son, watching my family and friends delighting in their gifts, thinking if ever my life had a moment of perfection, this was it.

But there were three more presents to give out. I fished the dragon scale out of my bag. In the candlelight, the blue scale was rimmed in a coppery glow. Holly's fat little fingers reached for it. She immediately stuck it in her mouth. The poor kid was teething.

Mason frowned. "It won't hurt her, will it?"

"It's fine." No tooth on Terra could break a dragon scale. "But we maybe should wash it first." I tugged the scale away. Holly cried out, but I distracted her with a new stuffed bear.

"And I have something for Jacoby too. It's not really a Christmas present, but I think this is a good time for it."

Jacoby looked up from where he was playing with his new widget.

"This is for you." I handed him a small booklet. I'd had to beg the bank manager for it. No one kept printed records of bank transactions anymore. This was old school. But I wanted something tangible for Jacoby to hold in his hands.

His gnarled fingers grasped the book. He flipped open the first page and saw the numbers printed there.

"Whats is it?"

"It's your salary. I told you an apprentice should be paid." I pointed to the first deposit. "That's your money for the work you've already done for me. Now, every week you will see more money in your account."

Jacoby hugged the bank book to his chest. "It's mine?"

"All yours."

"I buys cookies with it?"

"You can buy whatever you want, but you shouldn't spend it all on cookies."

Jacoby nodded.

"I'll show you how to access it on your widget, and we'll set up a budget for you."

"Budg…et?"

"That's where you decide how much money you should save and how much you can spend on cookies."

His face brightened. "Budget!" He ran off to show his prize to Raven and the others.

I turned to Mason. "This last gift is for us." I pulled out a small box wrapped in simple white paper and tied with a red bow.

"Who's it from?" Mason asked.

"Carmen. She wouldn't let me open it until I was home. She said that way I would have to share it with you."

"Intriguing. Open it."

"Together," I said. We both took hold of a ribbon and pulled. Holly helped us tear off the paper. Inside was a two-pound bag of coffee beans and a note:

A thank you to you, Kyra, for a job well done, and a thank you to Mason for letting us steal Kyra away during the holidays. Merry Christmas.

ICE SPRITES—AS CUTE AS THE YETI IS FIERCE

January 3, 2083

One more post this week before I get back to work and my life is turned upside down again. This one is along the same theme as the last post about Yetis—ice-sprites, the yeti's smaller, cuter cousins.

A few years ago, I found a little, wilted creature in the middle of the hot city. He was winged and covered in downy white fur. And he seemed to be struggling in the heat. Really struggling.

I have no idea how he got there. Probably some collector who decided he was too much work to care for. I took him home and tried to keep him cool while I figured out what he ate (anything sweet). It was a close thing. I didn't think he'd survive those first days. I nursed him through an especially hot July.

Those were the early days of my pest control business, and I barely had enough money to keep me and my few rescues fed. I spent every cent I had on bags of ice to keep the poor little guy cool. I wasn't even sure what he was at that time.

Eventually, he blossomed into a beautiful creature with wings, about the size of a snowy owl. I dubbed him as an ice-sprite and named him Kur because he makes a little chirping-purring noise that sound like he's saying "kurrrr."

I hand fed him all that summer and fall, until he was strong enough to fly. That winter, I brought him to Dorion Park to set him free, but he'd followed me back to my truck, sat on my windshield wipers and chirped until I let him in. That was eight years ago. He was one of my first rescues and my first foster fail. He's been with me ever since.

But lately, he's been looking a little wilted again. Not sick exactly, just sad. I took him on my last Inbetween adventure hoping the cold and abundance of fresh air would perk him up, and it did. But going forward, I wonder if Kur's diet could use some revamping. Does anyone out there in the blogosphere have experience with ice-sprites? What do you feed them?

COMMENTS (4)

You're asking the wrong question. Not what you feed it, but what you feed it to.

Biggameguy21 (January 3, 2083)

———•———

Ice chips?

Soupie (January 3, 2083)

———•———

We had a similar creature here. My dad called it a monkey-owl. He hung around for one winter and we never saw him again. I used to feed him bread, but he didn't seem too excited about it.

BetweenSteader (January 4, 2083)

———•———

First, I love your blog. Thanks for trying to care for all those creatures. As a biologist, zoologist and former vet tech, I have been studying what we used to call cryptids for the last 50 years. Now, of course, they have gone from myth to commonplace. That doesn't make them any easier to understand. I would say that if your ice-sprite craves sugar, that's probably what his body needs to survive. Good luck with all your foster fails!

YukonZookeeper (January 4, 2083)

Dear Reader,

There will be more Valkyrie Bestiary to come! The next books in the series will bring the focus back to Montreal where Kyra and Mason get caught up in the godling uprising and face off against other, darker villains. Don't miss out on Valkyrie Bestiary news. Be sure to join the reader's group at https://kimmcdougall. com/Readers-Group

I want to thank all the readers who have taken the time to send me emails or post reviews of the Valkyrie Bestiary books. *Oh, Come All Ye Dragons* was the most fun I've had writing in the Valkyrie Bestiary world so far. I'd love to hear what you thought of it too.

If you enjoyed this book I would be grateful for your honest review. And I'll try to make it as painless as possible. Visit the review page on my site at https:// kimmcdougall.com/review-oh-come-all-ye-dragons to leave a review on Amazon or your favorite review site.

Thank you for reading *Oh, Come All Ye Dragons,* and I hope to see you in the Inbetween again soon! In the mean time, if you need a romantic paranormal suspense fix, check out the snippet below from my other series, Hidden Coven.

Kim McDougall

ACKNOWLEDGMENTS

I have amazing readers! They are the best part about writing. I am always thrilled when readers reach out to say they enjoyed a book or a character or even if they had a little cry at certain parts (we all need a safe place to cry sometimes). My readers are also terrific at telling the world about Kyra and her critters, and I credit much of the series' success to that.

I'd like to thank a few of my Aussie readers in particular: Astra Felstead, Pat Ciszewski, April Tippett, and Kate Westaway all answered the call when I asked for help with some of the wording on Kyra's blog. I'm so glad that the Valkyrie Bestiary has found a home with Australian readers.

I'd also like to thank my cover artist, Kayla Schweisberger, who never bats an eye when I say things like, "I need a cute blue dragon wrapped in Christmas lights and a tiny yeti-like creature putting a star on his head." Kayla always says, "Sure!" and then proceeds to come up with something amazing. I don't know how you do it, but thank you.

None of the Valkyrie Bestiary books would happen without my editor and friend, Elaine Jackson. Over the past 10 books, Elaine has become my sounding board for new ideas, which means I write myself into corners much less frequently these days. Thank you, Elaine!

Finally, I'd like to thank my brilliant daughter, Genevieve Chatel, for her hard work with all the nitty-gritty stuff that comes with running a book publishing business, leaving me more time to write new books. And my husband, Louis Chatel, who told me years ago I should be writing what I love to read. And now I do.

Kim McDougall

DISCOVER KYRA'S WORLD

This story may be over, but Valkyrie Bestiary isn't done yet! Don't miss out on the latest new releases and other writing news. Join the VB Reader's Group at https://kimmcdougall.com/Readers-Group.

Want to find out more about Kyra's world?

Learn more about the Valkyrie Bestiary series and other books by Kim McDougall at https://kimmcdougall.com.

Poke around at Kyra's blog at http://valkyriebestiary.com.

Find all the Valkyrie Bestiary books (including prequels and novellas) along with deleted scenes and series FAQ at https://kimmcdougall.com/valkyrie-bestiary.

Other places you can follow Kim McDougall Books:

Facebook: https://www.facebook.com/KimMcDougallBooks

Instagram: https://www.instagram.com/kimmcdougallbook

Amazon: https://www.amazon.com/-/e/B002C7CI2M

Bookbub: https://www.bookbub.com/authors/kim-mcdougall

Goodreads: https://www.goodreads.com/author/show/1432797.Kim_McDougall

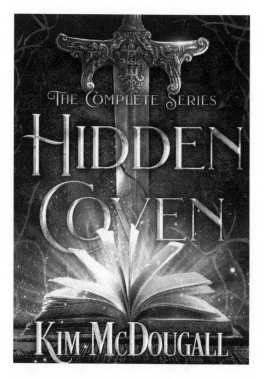

Quinn is cursed. Bobbi's a magical screw-up. Together they make a great pair.

As ley-lines swell, thinning the veil between worlds, the witches of Hidden Coven guard their most precious resource—magic.

Protected by dark wards and guided by a mad seer, the coven is still vulnerable to the attacks of a true demon intent on seizing the coven's power.

In this complete series of five novellas, Bobbi begins as a novice spell-caster, more powerful and dangerous than anyone guesses. She will have to become the warrior and protector that the divine Lady sees in her.

She'll lay her life on the line. She'll even question her sanity. Is it all worth it to save a coven that doesn't seem to want her?

Quinn has his own demons to fight, including his cold-hearted mother and a mystical illness that threatens to take him down. Together, Bobbi and Quinn confront the family secrets that set their story in motion long before they were even born.

Excerpt from *Hidden Coven*:

My will into fire. It was a simple spell. What could go wrong? I tilted my head, studying the three spell ingredients on the grass—an amethyst, a posy of fresh buttercups catching the last rays of sunlight, and a candle in a glass votive—all sitting with me inside a ring of salt. I had no idea if that was right. This was a seat-of-the-pants adventure.

Damn, it's humid.

A proper witch left her hair long and loose for rituals. Mine hung like a damp towel around my neck. The grimoire suggested spells were best done sky-clad, but public nudity made me self-conscious. Even in my secluded backyard, I wore a long t-shirt and panties.

I peeled the shirt from my damp skin and rearranged the ingredients again, laying the flowers across the amethyst. Buttercups were a visual aid to represent heat and light. The crystal would bend my sympathetic magic to ignite the candle and POOF! I'd have fire.

Light into heat, heat into flame.

I frowned at the wilted flowers. Did withered buttercups retain their affinity with the sun? Would a carnelian stone be better than the amethyst for fire magic? Maybe. I dithered and I knew it.

This was the problem with independent learning. I had no one to ask about the finer details of spell weaving. The only decent instruction book I'd found was Miss Abernathy's Grimoire, an ancient, hand-written tome of dubious origin. Miss Abernathy said to "use a crystal attuned to your spirit and the cycle of seasons." What the hell did that mean? How could I tell if a stone was attuned to me, let alone the season?

I sighed. The afternoon wore on toward dusk. The amethyst would have to do. At least it had grounding properties. If nothing else, I could use some grounding. This whole process left me jumpy.

Carefully, I poured more salt on the circle around me to keep out bad spirits. Better not to chance it. Not that I expected demons to be interested in my lowly attempt at magic, but Miss Abernathy's first rule of conjuring was "try your best and prepare for the worst," one of her frequent and slightly patronizing platitudes.

The ground was warm and damp under me with the loamy smell of recent rain. I crossed my legs and stretched the kinks from my neck before closing my eyes and trying to relax. Turning my mind inward, I pushed away hundreds of fledgling thoughts vying for my attention. My connection to the ground evaporated as I tuned out the itch of grass on calves and thighs. Waves of light and shadow swirled across the canvas of my closed eyelids, splitting and melding like breakers on a beach.

This has to work.

The number of near-disasters and odd coincidences in my life came to a head last month. I could still feel the strain of my clenched fists while Charles, my cheating ex-boyfriend, choked and clawed at his throat. I hadn't touched him, but his eyes bulged, and his face turned red before realization made me stop. I had done that to him.

That fiasco spurred me to finally take up the reins of my education into the dark arts.

Wrong thoughts.

I shoved Charles aside and focused on the sensation of my body parts dropping away one by one. My toes disappeared first, then my calves. A light breeze prickled my sweaty skin, breaking my concentration.

Deep breath in. I began again.

Goodbye toes, calves, thighs, shoulders...

My mind floated in a whorl of light and dark, free but anchored to the secret well inside me—a space between my heart and my womb where I imagined all my memories, hopes and dreams were stored. I dipped into that well, drawing on the power I found there.

I opened my eyes. The last rays of sun glinted off the crystal.

"Ignis." My voice rang like a church bell heard two counties away. The blood-red amethyst glowed. The rest of the world blurred and darkened as I looked down a long tunnel at the stone and posy.

Light into heat, heat into flame. Power of the sun into fire!

Something inside me broke, like the membrane around a yolk, spilling power through my veins.

"Ignis!" I shouted.

The amethyst gleamed. The flowers blackened and smoked.

Light into heat, heat into flame!

The candle wick sparked. A giddy surge of power washed over me. It was amazing. Exhilarating! Every fiber of my body tingled with a brilliant intoxication. I held up fingers that glowed from within. I was the fading twilight, even as I bathed in the twilight. I was the power. Magic rushed through me, flooding my veins, bolstering me until I felt like a leaf tossed on the wind. I laughed with pure joy.

Then the wind became a tornado.

Magic turned livid. Light flared with a white-hot screech. Pain shot through me. The candle shattered in an explosion of wax and glass, slashing me with dozens of tiny blades. But the pain went much deeper. This new force bit my soul, tore a piece of me away, and shredded my power.

I tried to scream but heard only a desperate gurgle from my throat. I couldn't move. The magic I'd unleashed thrummed, drowning out all sound and thought.

I tried to unlatch the razor-sharp tendrils biting into me, binding me to the magic. But they clung to my secret well. I'd laid open my sacred space, and it was now violated by power I couldn't control. I was caught, held tight in an invisible iron grip.

And it sucked my magic dry.

Frozen, I teetered back and hit the ground.

*

Hidden Coven, The Complete Series is now available at your favorite book retailer. Find it at https://kimmcdougall.com/hidden-coven.